THE BENEFITS OF TOBACCO

Shane Harrison was born in Dublin. He graduated from the National College of Art and Design in the early '80s and has worked in television, advertising and as a freelance designer. His first collection of short stories, *Blues Before Dawn,* was published by Poolbeg in 1992 and he has also contributed stories, articles and reviews to a range of newspapers and periodicals. He has a BA degree in English literature from Dublin City University and currently works as a librarian in County Wicklow. He lives in Bray with Marian and their two children, Oran and Davin.

SHANE HARRISON

The Benefits of Tobacco

To Gerlinde
best wishes
Shane Harris

First published in 2007
by Forty Foot Press
Box 10715, Glenageary, Co. Dublin, Ireland

Cover Design and Layout by A.J. Gatsby
Set in 11/14 pt Baskerville

Printed in Ireland by Central Press Ltd,
Bray, Co. Wicklow
Typeset by Helita Typeset, Bray, Co. Wicklow

A CIP record for this book
is available from the British Library
ISBN 978-0-9553597-1-2

To Oran and Davin

Acknowledgements

Acknowledgements are due to the editors of the following publications where these stories first approved:

The Madonna of the Streets was first published in *The Phoenix Anthology* (Editor: David Marcus,1999),

The Falling Dream was first published in *Writings Magazine* (1995),

Still Life With Seaweed was first published in *Stet* (1993),

See Emily Play was first published in *Stream and Gliding Sun* (Editor: David Wheatley, 1998),

Ante Meridian was first published in *Wildeside Magazine* (2001),

A Day, The Aeroplane Trap and *Big Blue Horizon* were published in *The Bray Arts Club Journal* (2001, 2003, 2004).

Thanks also to Abraxas, Anne Fitzgerald, Marian Osborne and my editor, Penelope Ireland.

Contents

Her Yellow Eyes   5

The Madonna of the Streets   13

The Ice Devil   23

The Falling Dream   33

Still Life with Seaweed   43

See Emily Play   49

Pushing the River   67

New Year's Eve   93

Ante Meridian   103

A Day   111

The Aeroplane Trap   121

The Benefits of Tobacco   125

Big Blue Horizon   135

The Apartment Opposite   139

The Benefits of Tobacco

*"A cigarette is the perfect type of a perfect pleasure —
it is exquisite and it leaves one unsatisfied.
What more can one want?"*

Oscar Wilde, The Picture of Dorian Gray

Her Yellow Eyes

TO be honest, I had forgotten about the whole affair. It was buried beneath the smut and grease of life, and even if I was to wipe away the accretions of time, down to the clear glass, well, what then? Louise had been my lover and then it was no more. I was a married man, happily, I would have said in the days before Louise, and silent, suffering Monica was still my wife. It was best to forget and never to turn when that perfume wafted past in the wake of another nameless body, best not to listen when a particular song played on the radio, best not to make comparisons.

There are few people with that loose-limbed walk, making the same slurred signature with their step. I know that step well, not quite suited to high heels, hesitant, but hesitant in the predatory sense. I saw the shapely legs and followed them up, recognising everything on the way; her auburn hair, her pale teardrop face, her yellow eyes.

I am a mechanic. I fix things. Mostly I fix cars for the not-so-rich. I fix their cars and sometimes, in the time-honoured hubbub of things, I get to fix their electrical appliances and other broken things they can't bring themselves to abandon. Nothing expensive or state-of-the art, just bric-a-brac that might otherwise lie about an attic rusting, or that might find its way at dead of night to an illicit dumping ground.

Louise had loved me like a waitress. So full of sincerity in my presence, served me what I liked, all that Italian food: fellatio and cunnilingus. Then she left, just upped and was gone and I never knew why. Maybe the tipping was too bad.

The Benefits of Tobacco

She smelled of cigarettes and sweet liqueur. She said "hi". I had prepared for such an eventuality, of course. I had analysed all the possibilities, considered each and every response. What would I be; diffident, sulky, devil-may-care, if she ever walked into my life again; with her auburn hair and teardrop face, her yellow eyes?

I stood and wiped my hands. I scanned the racks of tools hanging on the wall as though I would find a prompt. Swarfiga, I thought, Hilti gun, there was a calendar for Miss Rigid Tools, but best not to think of that.

"The view," she said, "must be pretty down there." She smiled and showed her imperfect teeth.

I asked what I could do for her and she said, in her flat, middleclass voice, that she could do with a service. I nodded at her car. I knew it. A black Ford Sierra I had sold to Sam, her common-law husband or whatever he was. No problem, I said, "No problemo." I must have decided on the devil-may-care response.

"That was a joke." she said, with a disconsolate swagger of her hips, "You've lost your sense of humour."

Well, I could have exploded, could have said, in my best scornful voice, "What gives you the right to waltz in here looking down your Roman nose? What gives you the right to act so superior after all these years, with your auburn hair, pale teardrop face, your yellow eyes?"

Instead I shrugged and mentioned that a sense of humour was not the only thing I had lost, and the losing was not something to break my heart.

"Oh well." she said, "I was just wondering."

I asked her if she wanted to lift her bonnet, but she demurred, not intimating whether she got the joke or not. She probably did. She was no less sharp than when I had

known her; that predatory look, the sharp teeth, keenly
focussed eyes scanning the terrain for prey.

"There's something else." she said.

Sam was a big wheel in advertising. He had those suits
with the turned up lapels, slicked back hair and regulation
ponytail, he had uncommonly broad shoulders and tiny
feet; really you would expect him to topple over if left
unattended. Perhaps that was the reason why Sam was
most comfortable when propped at some bar and why he
seemed never left unattended. His loyal friends; the
copywriters, lawyers, designers and second rate actors of
the advertising world were always there to prop him up.

Women fell readily for his pointed eyes, were entranced
by his deep and decadent mansmell. As they lurched with
him in the bowels of some latenight Leeson Street
basement they were reassured to feel in the infinitesimal
space between their still clothed bodies the hard, swelling
insistence of his throbbing wallet.

So why did Sam marry Louise? If he did marry her. So
far as I could see, she was little more than a fashion
accessory. She went with his charcoal pinstripe, comple-
mented his colourless smile with the fire of her auburn
hair, her teardrop face, her yellow eyes.

Why did I fall in love with her? Or she with me? If she
did fall in love with me.

It was to do with mechanics. You need a mechanic you
can trust. To the common man, or woman, what lies
beneath the bonnet is a sublime mystery. When it works it
is pure faith, when it doesn't it becomes a beast, a snarling
and vindictive brute.

I had gone to the same school as Sam though we didn't
rub blazers. He was amongst the ranks of the high

achievers. We frequented the same pool halls where Sam cut a dash in his suit and waistcoat, moving, again, in different circles.

Louise lies back on the green baize and says she is a snooker widow. She spreads her legs and sighs and closes her yellow eyes. The hall fades into darkness as I chalk my cue and climb aboard. I enter her and she moans.

"Shouldn't you keep one foot on the floor?"

But that was then and this is now. We warily circled the car, Louise and I. I asked about this and that, the state of the weather, her health; oh, and by the way, how's Sam?

Her eyes were averted. She looked down into the garage pit.

"That hole." she began, then paused. "That hole in the ground, what's it called?"

"The pit." I said.

"That bad?"

I told her that I was selling out and moving up. House prices were hysterically high and I couldn't resist the urge to dispose of the property and retreat to the solitude of the West. It was a romantic vision, I had no notion of pragmatic concerns; but Monica surrendered to it all. The sameness of our life was so sad that anything should yield an improvement.

The pit was the problem. The buyers baulked at the notion of buying anything with a hole. They had kids, they insisted, they had a life.

"I have to fill it in." I said. "Next week at the latest."

"The pit and the pendulum." Louise said and her yellow eyes burned with avid interest.

The Black Sierra had been a favourite of mine. I remember Sam had been at college then, just another impecunious jerk. He was doing a diploma in business studies or something, he was eaten alive with acne. Having received his diploma, as much for the acne as the acumen, he decided that he needed a car. So the Black Sierra that had once been mine became his. A bit like what happened with Louise.

We were made for each other, Louise and I. Monica and I were all sharp edges and crashing gears; Louise and I were the perfect fit. Then one day I found myself plummeting earthwards and heard her laughter from the clouds. Perhaps Sam's discreet charm had reclaimed her, perhaps she just grew restless, perhaps.

There is a special room she had built for Sam. She had it designed like a sophisticated lounge, with a small bar, a neon executive toy and a half size snooker table. She got the idea from a country and western song and reckoned that it might help to keep Sam at home some nights. Any night.

Louise slinks around the den. She lifts the cue and adopts that pose of James Dean from Giant. She lies back on the green baize and spreads her legs and sighs and closes her yellow eyes. The hall fades into darkness as some man, any man, emerges from a corner and chalks his cue. She tells him to keep one foot on the floor and laughs, lasciviously, at her own joke.

"I suppose." I say to Louise, "That Sam is still moving up, I always knew he'd go far."

"Not so far." she says. "Not far at all."

I tell her that I had seen him in Pembroke Street a month ago. I heard the call and turned to see the red Beamer and Sam's firm jaw wearing a customer greeting grin.

The Benefits of Tobacco

"He's looking well." I say, to little reaction. "He never seems to grow any older."

"How true." she says.

"I suppose though, he wouldn't be caught dead in an old Ford."

"You would be surprised." she says, "Where one might find our Sam."

We arrive at the boot. Our eyes flicker from the chrome fittings to each other.

"The Ford?" I prompt.

"Sam left it to me."

"Left it?"

"Left me too." she says.

The boot creaks open. I stare but am afraid to look and see the eyes stare, sightless, back at me. My lips move with profane, vernacular prayers, I call to the dusty, falling stillness of the garage to witness the truth. My God, sweet Jesus and the saints. I turn my frozen face to see her apply more gloss and surreptitiously moisten her lips.

I remember the black jokes we whispered to each other in dark suburban bars. I see the ghastly orange lights, the swirling carpets of coiled serpents, and I feel her lips close to my ear. "Kill her." she said, "Kill silent, suffering Monica."

It was all hypothetical, of course. A titbit to feed the mind, in the drunken, lingering interval before feeding desire. "Like in the movies." I said. "Shouldn't we kill Sam first."

Everything was yellow under the lounge lights. Her pale yellow face, her dark yellow hair. She closed her eyes and wore a deathmask for a while. "I'll look after the blood." she said, "If you take care of the burials."

Her Yellow Eyes

There are times when I would have done it, there really are. But those times are gone. I am of the walking wounded with no remorse for what I've done but a cold clenching fear for what I might have done.

It is the final scene of our film noir. Sam is neatly stained through the heart but otherwise well turned out. It's funny how much he weighs, even with his wallet removed. We lay him in the pit.

"Shouldn't we say something." I say.

She crouches down, elegantly, above the pit. Her face blank, no teardrops in her yellow eyes. She smiles and says, "Please don't ever change."

It was a reasonable deal. She would keep my secret if I kept hers. That, and fill the hole with cement. Silent, suffering Monica smiled hugely when I told her we would leave some days early.

"It will be a new beginning." she said and sighed.

"A new beginning." I said.

I closed the garage door for the last time. I had stood there when Louise drove away, had waved at her rear view mirror although she did not respond in kind. There was nothing wrong with the black Sierra. Although, as it faded into the distance something uneven caught my ear. Worn tappets, I figured; she'll need to get that seen to.

The Madonna of the Streets

THE high arched roof of the arcade was set with thick squares of opaque glass that never told the colour of the sky, but they did serve to amplify any light that chanced above the city and on bright days would glare down painfully like suns. The whole arcade, in fact, functioned like an amplifier for the elements. On hot days it had the swelter of the Casbah, other days it would host visiting winds from Siberia or Archangel, on busy days shoppers' footfalls, hawkers' cries and buskers' songs mingled in the tunnel and rose to an unbearable din.

The canopy did keep the rain at bay, at least for those who had their pitch a reasonable distance from the towering entrance portals. Rafe was not one of those; being newly back in town he had to content himself with the margins – time, muscle and talent would eventually change that. As for now he huddled deeper into his duffel coat, pulled up the hood and waited, waited like a monk for alms.

The place had come to remind him of an airport, having that same strange cocktail of anticipation and boredom, of comings and goings; but it was one airport where he seemed unable to book a flight out. He had once said that to Jenny, in the long, hurt postamble to their relationship.

"A bit like life." she had said.

He had been unprepared for pathos; "Life is like an airport?"

"No. Like waiting for a flight out." But she wasn't going to argue, she had smiled in the pause then patted his ruffled brow; "It doesn't matter."

13

The Benefits of Tobacco

Rafe still had these conversations with her inside his head, looking for the clue, the one rough grain of sand that would lodge in the waist of the hourglass and arrest time's ceaseless downward flow. Or simply searching for a last rebuttal to leave him vindicated, as he did now, baring his teeth in a hollow laugh at what he should have said to that.

A passerby gave him a worried nod and then, as an afterthought (or perhaps to prevent this leering man from following him) dropped a coin in the chalk circle at Rafe's feet. The coin sang briefly, though more sweetly than its tuppence worth deserved, and this reminder of commerce brought him back to earth. Meanwhile, at the far entrance arch, Dave the busker struck up Memphis Blues Again.

It was one of his best Madonnas, ochre and umber, opalescent white highlights dancing on her skin, almond eyes that looked down gently on the child who was just an outline in her arms. There was only one thing missing; to be accurate it was twice missing, but it was one deliberate omission.

"Where is the halo on the Virgin?"

Rafe was sorely tempted to make a crude reply to that question, but the gaunt-faced priest would probably not have understood the word. Besides, the holy man was shabby, streetworn, so there was a vague kindred between them that demanded respect.

"The Holy Family, young man," the words wheezed from purple lips, "must - always - have - a - halo." He raised a bony finger heavenward for emphasis and Rafe's eyes meekly followed. Perhaps the canopy would have transformed itself into an echo of the Sistine Chapel, a ceiling alive with celestial beings carried aloft on the columns of commerce while the workaday streetnoise became a heavenly choir. But it remained blank, pitilessly modern and devoid of all meaning.

Rafe's eyes fell back to his Madonna. He knew what he had drawn on the pavement, even an inkling of why he had drawn it, crouched till he thought his back would snap; if anyone deserved a halo it was himself. Not her, certainly not around that guileful and beautiful face which had its own radiance and didn't require any ethereal lampshade.

"It is complete." Rafe said, and then, with a veiled hint, "And she is only a poor Madonna on the street."

The priest huffed at this, "She would shed a tear, then; down here among the sinners."

Perhaps the priest would have preferred, Rafe thought, those kitsch and sentimental paintings sold in cheap stores; gilt framed paintings of street urchins with one giant crystal tear poised on their baby cheeks. Picturesque poverty to be found only in rambling minds, not here, in this alley, where snot nosed beggars could swipe his day's takings if he wasn't careful... "There's no room for halos here." was all he muttered.

But the priest only smiled, as though he understood, and his fondness for Rafe's Madonna seemed to grow. Rafe looked at him in amazement, he knew then what the priest was going to do and there was no way of stopping it. There would be no donation but, in his own priestly way, the man of the cloth was staking claim to the work: stepping back a pace but managing to remain an island in the throng, he solemnly blessed the mother and child and then, without fuss, faded from the arcade.

Rafe was left with a truly holy picture, a fact that did not appeal to him too much. There was a chancer who frequented the arcade peddling cigarette-card pictures of the saints – "Holy picture, sir; holy picture, miss." was his monotonous and wheedling refrain. He was able-bodied, young, well kitted out – he was capable; but posing as a beggar he could rival Rafe's takings for the day with negligible effort.

"Here, why don't you paint me a Virgin and I'll show you how to sell her?" he had first joked by way of introduction. Rafe had told him where he intended inserting such a chalked paving slab and that had put an abrupt end to any potential friendship. They remained on sneering terms. But maybe he should have employed the Holy Picture Man as his marketing manager, since he frequently found that his takings were in inverse proportion to the quality of his work.

He brushed at his slab, as though checking for any damage it might have suffered in the blessing. It was still whole, she still shone on him – perhaps this latter fact was what kept his chalk ring so nearly empty; he was painting for himself, not for them.

Dave was still singing Dylan. *"One more cup of coffee,"* he moaned, *"one more cup of coffee 'fore I go, to the valley below."*

He would kill Dave, that one brought it all back and he remembered they had even thrown coins at the busker to get him to play it again. How many coffees had he and Jenny drunk together? In plastic cups from the clapped out machine in the Art College common room, greasy with cream in Buswell's as they laughed at floridly drunk politicians, or in Bewley's as group arguments raged over the meaning of art, of life, of all the things of which they knew nothing. And coffee gone cold in his ragged bedsit as they made love in front of a long dead fire...

It was raining now and the first umbrellas pirouetted above the crowd in the street outside like a drunken black ballet. A gusting wind blew spray to where Rafe crouched and he cursed, there was no point in continuing with this. Better to take the busker's advice. He scraped petulantly at the coins in his circle, his numbed fingers barely able to gather the smaller change of his miserable bounty. Enough for a coffee or two, or a coffee and a scone – and then a fifty pence piece clattered onto the ground beside him.

It belonged, had belonged, to a pair of Doc Marten's, a new pair of Doc Marten's. He had first seen them yesterday on the feet of the Holy Picture Man and now realised, with black mirth, that he had sunk to such depths that he could recognise people by their shoes.

"Happy Christmas." The Holy Picture Man was lording it, it had been a good day for selling saints.

"And a prosperous New Year." Rafe said, mildly, as he placed one knee over the coin in a form of genuflection.

The Holy Picture Man shoved both hands deeper into his pockets, lewdly jingling his change. "Tell me," he asked, "What do you call her?"

"The Madonna of the Streets."

"Not the Virgin on the Rocks?" He smirked at his own little joke. "I was just curious. But the child, you haven't given a name to the child..."

Rafe darkened, his body clenched. The Holy Picture Man was no fool, he backed off a pace and took a hand from his pocket to raise it in a pacifying gesture. "I was just curious." Then, ever the jester, he took the wad of pictures from his other pocket and, fanning them, held them out to Rafe. "Pick a card." he said, "Any card." Rafe wasn't playing and so he flicked one, seemingly at random, landing it on Rafe's knee – the one covering the coin.

It landed face down and Rafe, always ready for the sign, took his eyes off his tormentor and picked up the card. The Holy Picture Man took this opportunity to slope off towards the street, leaving Rafe to glare after him. He had turned over the picture, it was St. Jude, patron saint of lost causes.

Happy Christmas? It was the end of November but already the good cheer mob was limbering up. As Rafe pocketed his money and left the arcade he heard the loudspeaker of a nearby record shop give tidings of comfort and joy.

Comfort and Joy.

He would not look back, he must escape from that face, that thing in her arms; everything that slumbered and festered in the past. If the wind blew in more rain it would melt that image, but that had been the case before and still he had returned to the same spot to see her ghost, their ghosts, cling palely to the ground at his feet. Waiting, waiting for his hands to etch colour into their contours, breathe life into them as if he was Prometheus on the river bank.

Like all artists he lived vicariously through his work, or else transferred his experience to the images he wrought, but obliquely, hiding the trail from even himself. Either way life became something that passed him by, for, even if he sometimes chewed on the finer cuts of life, life itself, that bloated beast, could graze or gallop far beyond him, into meadows which he would never reach. It was he, Rafe, who was the grain of sand lodged in the waist of the hourglass, and in all this time spent smouldering on a broken dream a year had passed.

God rest ye merry gentlemen
and listen while I say
That Mary's boychild Jesus Christ
was born on Christmas Day...

It was the damp chill at which November excels, yet Rafe remembered the wait as being suspended in a globe of sunshine. Perhaps that was because there were Cordiline trees in the garden adjacent to the doctor's house, shaking their shaggy heads like palm trees on a beach; and a white wooden veranda that came straight from Regency days – all conspired to make him feel cocooned from that cold and windy day as he awaited the tidings of Jenny's visit.

...Tidings of Comfort and Joy...

And the dusty boards on which he walked opened like a trapdoor over a chasm as he saw Jenny rush towards him. She was eight weeks gone and the baby would arrive in the high, high summer of July. They hugged, two drowning people holding on for love and terror in the barren ocean; suddenly, what seemed to have shrivelled up and died was now ubiquitous and spoke its name again at every corner, echoed in every footfall and rustled in every leaf.

So even Rafe, the cynic and the swaggart, mellowed into smiles and radiated the true strength of giving and contentment. This was when he had first begun his Nativity scenes, by way of thanks, in humility, in all honesty. He had borne the scorn of friend and foe, who jibed that he had found Jesus, or that Jesus had found him; but it was someone else, inside himself, that he had found.

And inside Jenny a universe, a spiral galaxy moved and

threw an arm outward against the blackness.

      ... *Joy.*

The last note sank dull and discordant as Rafe pushed through the door of Bewley's Oriental Cafe and clumped, almost blindly, across the tiled floor of the foyer. It was hot and he felt unwell. The displays of handmade sweets and chocolates along one wall seemed impossible, a bad surrealist joke in this empty-bellied city, and he steadied himself against the brass rail of the self-service counter until the colours died down a pace.

An old woman nudged his elbow: "Follow the queue, love." He followed, meekly, took a sticky bun from the shelf because it was convenient and ordered coffee from the girl.

He looked around for a face he might know amongst the poets and the plotters and the office girls, but there was no-one and everyone. Jumbled and spinning like the faces on coins the priest, The Holy Picture Man and Dave the busker were hunched over coffees and sniggering at their connivance in bringing him here. At a table in the corner, alone and sullen, sat Jenny.

"I've booked a flight out." she said, with the same eerie melancholy with which she always said it.

Rafe said nothing, stirring brown sugar from sachets into the frothy mess.

"There's no future for us. We're hiding from it, hiding from our ..." But her words trembled and would not come.

"I'm sorry." he said, and in taking the blame had locked them forever in the past. Her image shimmered and dissipated, and outside, above the arcade, a sliver of rainwater found its way through a chink in the glass and fell towards the pavement below.

The Madonna of the Streets

If only he had told her to her face that he was sorry and so much more, or maybe the trouble was that his eyes had said it a million times. When first she had bled, on New Year's Day, he had felt that pip of dread grow to a stone, then a fist as they both slumped wounded about the flat for a week. Then, just when hope seemed bolstered by time, it had happened; the red and tiny, useless birth, like a parcel of liver on a butcher's table.

They had been methodical, calm; placing the remains in a glass jar which they wrapped in a swaddling of plastic bags. She had held it close, beneath her coat, on the slow and painful walk to the hospital, wordless, handing it like a gift to the nurse when they reached the ward. Then Rafe had stood in the comfortless waiting room, the bare bulb hanging dead, the only light a moonlike glow through the glass hatch from the next room and the sparkling tips of numerous cigarettes.

A nurse had placed the glass jar in the hatch window and for a while its red lantern glow had held him fascinated, then he longed for them to take it and, finally, turned away. Out over the rooftops and chimney stacks, the jungle of television aerials, he searched out the stars that held the sky in place, and waited for a falling star, and waited...

It was over now, he was sorry – and still the buzz inside his head accused him. The priest leered past: "Mea culpa, mea culpa, mea maxima culpa" and pointed to the ceiling where saints swirled and looked sombrely down. He recognised Saint Jude whose face came closer, "I've given up on you." he said and, laughing, turned into the Holy Picture Man.

"You've got to give the child a name." he said, and held out a card with Rafe's own likeness on it in the style of an icon. "A name, you've got to give it a name."

"And a halo." added the priest, "And a tear."

"If you give it a name it will all be over, like a disappearing universe it will swirl back to nothing at its cusp. It will be complete."

Rafe searched desperately for Jenny's face, somewhere in the crowd or in his mind, but she was gone and he could not conjure her up again. His eyes felt hollow, fastening onto nothing until they found the priest's glaucous eyes. Holding the stare until they were alone in the cafe Rafe felt himself dwindle in size to the slightness of a boy while the priest grew and grew until he loomed over him like a huge granite statue. Slowly the priest raised his right arm in blessing; "It's all over now." he soothed.

Rafe shut his eyes and recalled the earlier scene in the arcade, the blessing dropped on his precious drawing, all the rage he had nurtured welled up inside him and...

"Never!" he banged the table and felt the ensuing silence as poets and plotters and office girls turned to look at the wild man exploding. Rafe's eyelids snapped open to reveal to him the world he knew, or once knew, and he smiled as he saw their stares dip and avoid him as the murmur grew louder to hide their embarrassment.

Outside it was raining heavily and the streets were emptying as the crowds evaporated like mist. On the high arched roof of the arcade the rain flowed in a steady rivulet through the crack in a square of thick glass. It fell endlessly to the floor below, a solid silver rod piercing heaven and earth. Where it fell there had been a chalk circle with 'Thank You' written in neat serifed letters and beside that, worked exquisitely in chalk, a Madonna and child. It was one of his best Madonnas, ochre and umber, the child an outline in her arms...

The Ice Devil

THERE was a triangular room, very small, with a window and a heavy enamel sink. There was a girl, I remember there was a girl, but that would be much later. In this, the first tableau, a boy, a young man really, bends over the sink while another youth washes his hair. It is like that Hockney painting and the time, the era, is about right; their hair is long.

A net curtain, cheap and tatty, obscures the tableau from any prying eyes in the cobblestone square below, and inside, with the steam rising from the sink and the rinsing jug, I cannot clearly make out the features. But I know that I am one of the duo, not the one whose hair is wet and who is naked, the other one, the fair one.

All this happens in the apex of a triangular room, in slow-motion and seen through a tasteful soft focus lens. That is the way the past happens for me, like some trailer for an old arthouse movie, leaving faint but indelible images which I cannot shake loose from my head.

I remember all the deadmen stacked like skittles in the bedroom, each night they would grow in number and rattle their ghostly chains reproachfully next dawn. From the window in the bathroom, the only window, you could on a clear day with a relatively clear head see the Sacre Coeur.

All the photographs I have from then are of the Sacre Coeur, almost all. Bren feeding pigeons in the park, Bren dead drunk upon the grass, and stripped to the waist lighting votive candles in the dark. There are others of the great ice cream domes, stark against a cloudless sky, there are some of the Place du Tertre – including the tramp who wanted to be paid for walking into my frame, and a good many of dark complexioned people whose names I don't perfectly remember. And there is the girl; the girl I kissed and stung my hand amongst the briars – but I don't perfectly remember, it was a long, long time ago.

There is a little bit of the Ice Devil in us all, it lies there sleeping. Whatever else you may say about Bren, he was the one who invented the Ice Devil. It was there before, of course, but he gave it a name, made it real. So it lives on, out there somewhere and inside here, deep within each of us.

I remember.

There was a group of them and they were all friends of Yves. In fact, in that jungle hidden in the city, under the lazy heat of the sun, they could have been friends of everybody. We drank some liquor with them and it was hairy and coarse; the name sounded like shoeshine, and it tasted like that too. But the effect was pure honey so that when I look back on it I think of myself lying in a field of tall corn and the sky goes on forever, and always golden.

The field was full of dock and weeds, and buzzed with large and self confident insects of shapes I had never seen before and whose memory I cannot shake off. It was ringed by highrise towers. I see the black man sit cross legged at the head of the circle, he had that power, and light up a spliff the size of an ice cream cone. The rest is very hazy indeed.

But I know that is where I met the girl. I can feel the delicate bones of her hand move softly in my grip. We were alone together but nothing else comes, not yet.

Bren had learned that the supermarket sold beer by the can, very cheap, only that it was not very strong. Oh yes, from the start I saw the devil in his eye. The only trouble was that Yves did not have a fridge.

When I think of it I am sure that I must be making it up, that my mind is running some forgotten black comedy through my subconscious, making believe that we were the actors. It is all subtitled, of course, but I could swear that Bren, in that soft, brimmed hat, looks like Jean Paul Belmondo.

We found the fridge in an alleyway off Pigalle. I remember the smell of food, more hot dogs and grease than haute cuisine; and I remember the tempting heat from doorways where women lounged, dark skinned and almost naked, cigarette tips flaring by their mouths then falling down like shooting stars. There were a lot of football supporters on the street, full of lust and malevolence, and les flics swept by at regular intervals to dampen spirits and extinguish lights. We were searched twice and on neither occasion did they find the black man's burden, the ice cream cone factory. The devil was watching out for us even then and after the second search he revealed himself to us, alone in the newly darkened alley, the bulbous white monolith of the deserted fridge.

Bren took a photograph, of course, he would always take a photograph. He made Yves and I pose as he set the timer; so we three remain, frozen in sepia monochrome on a Paris street, reverently grouped around a discarded fridge.

The girl had said that my hands were cold. She didn't sound like she was complaining. Long and cold, she said, like Jack Frost. Perhaps that came from carrying that damned fridge through streets and through the Paris Metro; or maybe it was the Ice Devil, who always lived before all of this happened, a virus in my veins. So, there in the fields somewhere out past Viry Chatillon, we froze to ice, two statues entwined and bound by glittering spiders' webs; but yet her skin was melting – I know that, at least.

Spiders' webs. It's funny that I should think of them at a time like this. Spiders' webs are only magical in child-hood, after that there is something menacing about them. They become calculated, inexorable; portents of the patient, poised menace that is time.

We had been friends from school, Bren and I. I remember us walking together on Spring mornings, the myriad webs hanging like hammocks in the dark hedgerows; sleeping, shining hammocks that were there just to catch the dewdrops and sparkle. It was Bren who suggested that we drink the raindrops hanging from the railings. All along by the park we would stop to taste the acrid water and metal. It is much better this way, he said; but couldn't say why.

She was called Zsa Zsa, the girl was; what a stupid name. I knew that she was fond of me, but that she feared and lusted for Bren, as a beautiful moth for a fast burning candle. We three were all together again just once, some days after the day in the fields – the day of the long chillums.

I must have told Bren the story that my father had told me. Or perhaps he had been there in the gloomy brown pub, my old man holding court in that room of long-faced men with brimmed hats, pulling on pipes and long-necked bottles.

It was the Applejack story and he told it many times.

There were similar stories about Johnny-Jump-Up and other illicit booze, but it is the Applejack story which is relevant here. Listen to my father speak, listen to the Old Devil.

"Did I ever tell you boys about the lumberjack's drink, a fighting drink if ever there was?" And he waited while his pipe built up a head of smoke.

Then he began his tale and took us, through the windows of his grey eyes, into the Yukon Territory of Northern Canada; into a country of loggers and trappers and howling wolves – and piercing cold winters. You would swear he had been there, this man who had never left Ireland, but still his words chilled the beer in our bellies.

"A few bottles of redeye brought along would do nicely over Winter, but come Spring and they'd have the cider ready. They would have left the apples fermenting in barrels since the Fall, sugar and water was all they needed. And it made the purest cider with the surest kick. You've heard tell of the man who shot electricity into my walls?"

We had.

There was a sting in the tail, in each and every Eden there always is. And as that serpent offered ecstasy and damnation to Adam and Eve, so too did the Ice Devil coil around those decaying apples in the Yukon, his fangs prepared to strike.

"They called it Applejack, it was lumberjack's cider, but they could have branded it with the skull and crossbones. It could get out of hand if the weather got too cold, and it froze something mighty in the Yukon Territory."

This time the old man's story concerned a party of loggers from British Columbia, but all nationalities had featured in his tellings of the tale, wild Irish rovers to

The Benefits of Tobacco

Chinamen.

"You'll know from your science that alcohol freezes at a lower temperature than water, there's no freezing the demon. So this Spring, when the boys opened the barrels they saw ice, thick enough to dance on but not solid to the bottom. Had they been patient men they would have waited for the thaw and let the juices run together, but cooped up in log cabins over long dark nights and you don't half build up a thirst.

"The short of it is that they took a spike to the ice 'till they struck the gold that lay beneath, siphoned it off into jugs and settled down to some serious drinking. I'm telling you, there was electricity in their veins that night.

"When the trading party found them it was weeks later. It must have been a grisly sight. There had been seven loggers and they were all there to greet the trading party in the small clearing between the cabins. But there was something strange about them, not one of them moved nor raised a hand in greeting. Some were seated and others slouched against log piles or barrels, one stood leaning against an open cabin door; they were all quite dead. Dead and frozen, their beards and hair whitened in a web of frost so that they resembled wizened old men, their mouths open as though shouting – and no sound came or would come again."

That one time we were all together again, Bren and Zsa Zsa and I, we spent much of the night outside a small cafe near Yves' flat, drinking green liquor and not getting on too well. Bren had been conjuring up the Ice Devil with the cheep beer and the freezer compartment of the fridge and suggested we crack it open that night. At first we agreed, he said that he had tried it once before and that it was the smoothest set of wheels on the road between heaven and hell. If it was anyway wild at all, Bren would always insist that it was the best.

We hung back, of course, Zsa Zsa and I, and wrestled like lovers through streets and alleyways. We had no eyes for Bren, at least I didn't, except to laugh when an old prostitute put her bags down and called to him: "voulez vous?" Shortly afterwards we lost him in our kisses, lost ourselves and lost the city too. It was somewhere in the daze of morning that my footsteps clacked out as I cut diagonally across the cobblestone square.

I see it now from so many angles and nothing ever stays the same. I see it from outside and below and there remains one window lit in the square as the last lamplight flickers and dies, the light of the triangular room. But the glass is heavily condensated and I cannot decipher the silhouette that flickers there.

Then I am in the room and I approach the figure near the sink. It is difficult to see through the steam but I see that she is naked. I told you there is always a girl. As we embrace I look over her shoulder and see a figure walk into the square below. He is whistling and twirls into a mock dance as he approaches the plane trees beneath our window. Just once he pauses and leans rakishly against a lamppost. He has all the charm and allure of a thief and, knowing this, I hold the girl's face tight against my breast so that she will not see him. I cannot see his face beneath the brim of his felt hat but I can see the sparkle in his eyes as he catches my gaze. I know that look, its jaunty contempt for safety and control; a gauntlet thrown down before fate. Then he saunters away to disappear beneath the trees, leaving only that whistled melody to linger on.

The Benefits of Tobacco

It is the final tableau and now it is dark. Radio static hisses in the air and I hear the low whistle build to the sound of a kettle boiling. The smell of something sweet and sickly pricks the air and as I crouch, fearing danger, my hand sticks to something damp and warm. There is a glutinous stain, darker than the blackness and I pull my hand away.

I notice the faint blue light as I make for the kitchen and the sound of the rushing steam. The Ice Devil is peeping from the slightly open door of the refrigerator, and in that garish quarter light I see something that freezes the blood in my veins. Bren is crouched on the floor like a cat about to spring, and between his hands, or paws, the kettle spouts steam at his unprotected skin. He wears a grin of agony and I realise that in all the heat it is frozen there, as sure and cold as ice. And I see how dark he is and how dark and lifeless are his eyes. He has also cut himself so that blood glistens darkly in the sweat, and even as I suspect that Bren doesn't live here anymore, or at least that I no longer recognise him, I notice that he is aware of me just the same.

Turning those black eyes on me he says:

"I'm going to kill this thing, don't you see? I'm going to scald the ice from the bastard's soul, if I have to follow it to hell and be damned!"

It was not a time for reasoning, but a time for cool self-preservation. After all, who was to know just where the Ice Devil lurked, now that he was sprung from his vessel? He could live in the static or in the steam, in the very blackness of the air at night; he could live inside you or I, even within the righteous. And there inside these thoughts that I cannot shake off, I remain conscious of a presence, a face emerging from the shadows on the ceiling as I wait for the breaking of the day. I close my eyes and breathe. The picture is clear. I see him curled up and smiling in his sleep and I know, yes I know, that there is a little of the Ice Devil in us all.

The Falling Dream

IT was the falling dream awoke me. My old friend the falling dream. Whereas most people fall asleep, I, being peculiar, fall awake. I am spreadeagled and the wind whistles in my ears, a monochrome landscape rushes up to meet me. I dream in monochrome; that is something of a disappointment to me, although it does help to mitigate the vividness.

It was only a dream.

We live in a black and white film, Dermot and I. Or a film noir. I like that: film noir. Cafe noir. Dermot thinks that I am very pretentious; Grace is so arty farty I can hear him say, but then that is what he loves in me. Protecting me from reality, his woman of the floating world. He is a dentist, a dentist stroke businessman; rich and lovable?

There was a dream in a film I saw at college, very grainy and arthouse but beautifully weird. A manic film. First you see the moon and then the eye of a man. Then a thin sliver of cloud passes across the face of the moon and, while somebody holds the man's eye wide open, a razor blade is drawn across the iris. There is blood. You bet, black blood. Or at least I think so; it is a long time ago and it was a very old film, and anyway it was only a dream.

I doubt if Dermot ever dreams. He is much too real for such frivolity. He never shimmers in the changing light but maintains his own relentless solidity; the same solid, wavy hair, the same brown eyes, the same blue chin. If he smiles it is at my foolishness, though always in the most patient

33

and solid of ways. He is as much a rock to which I am bound as he is a partner. But I suppose in his own world he could be bound to a rock, alone, and each dawn an eagle flies to him and slowly, methodically, pecks out his liver.

It is dawn and I scream silently as I awake in sweat from the falling dream. Dermot is gone. On the bedside locker a cup of cold coffee lies, white scum stagnating on the liquid's surface. He has left it there for me, the coffee not the scum.

I rerun the last reel of the dream, scribbling notes on the pad I keep beneath my pillow. I must remember these things, they are significant. Very pretentious of me; very arty, I hear Dermot say. But I must remember.

We were in a city of white marble. Great buildings, heroic in their scale, stood guard over deserted canyon streets. Ragged birds circled overhead, ravens perhaps, or eagles.

We stood before the steps of a gothic cathedral, incongruous in this most spiritless place. We kissed, embraced – profanely. He moved down along my body. I felt his mouth on the skin of my abdomen, biting, and closed my eyes to let the passion lift me up, and up. Oh, and up.

I was in the campanile amidst the dull tolling of the bells and the lewd goading of the ragged birds.

It is all black and white, they must be ravens.

I leant over the parapet, dizzy from the height and the noise and the passion, saw Dermot emerge from the portals far below and descend the steps to the street. It is all black and white and he is wearing clothes like those worn in the films of the forties; brimmed hat with band, loose suit, like a Hollywood hood.

At the bottom of the steps thin human shadows were cast on the path, waiting for him. I tried to call above the bells and the birds but no sound came, then all noise ceased as the campanile dissolved into air and I plummeted down and down and...

On a morning such as this I should take a lover. Someone sordid and unclean and in every way very unlike Dermot. He could be the window cleaner perhaps, with no fear of heights, and I could trace his angular form in the mist I breathe upon the pane.

At first he might surprise me; stepping casually through the bathroom window to borrow a towel to wipe his grimy hands. I would be wearing the towel at the time, of course. Then, later, we would climb the ladder and make love on the roof.

Maybe not. I have no fear of heights, oh no – none at all; but the neighbours might object.

Dermot is gone, he has gone to work. He is a dentist and works inside people's mouths all day. He is very good at his job, he loves it very much. Why then does he take so little interest in my mouth and the thoughts and dreams that flow out of it?

I should take a lover but instead I take some Valium and dream a lot. I bet that he has a lover. I bet she lies back on his couch and that he holds her delicate jaw between index finger and thumb, he then bends forward to whisper in her seashell ear: open wide.

I close my eyes and dream the dream slowly forward. I dream his other hand free to bring the drill between her parted lips and come to rest above her wisdom tooth, there to wait, just wait. And when the panting stops...

The house is quiet. Dermot has his practice in town and I often wish he would bring it here and add some noise, even the occasional scream would be better than this.

There was a film on the television the other night. A Nazi dentist and a man in a tracksuit who was always in a hurry to get somewhere – rather like Alice's rabbit. Wherever he ran, though, he always seemed to end up back at the dentist's.

It was clear that the dentist wanted to get something out of him, and I don't mean teeth. That something, I learned between fitful bouts of sleep, was diamonds. Not that the diamonds were inside the man's mouth, oh no, and he had no gold teeth either. But if the dentist could drill into a healthy root without using an anaesthetic, he felt sure the man would tell him where the safe that held the diamonds was.

The running man screamed, oh how he screamed, but he said nothing.

Eventually the running man tricked the dentist and got him around to his place. It was a strange house, like a castle tower drowned in a lake. They stood facing one another on a metal dais above the water. Steps led down to the water. Then he gave the dentist the diamonds, the only snag was that the dentist had to eat them – one by one.

Who are these shadow people who come for Dermot when he is in the city? Are they ravens? Or eagles?

Dermot keeps a good supply of drugs at his surgery. This I know. Yes, and those drugs are a medium for beautiful dreams. Just think, all the dreams that money can buy. But sleep is uneasy when shadows creep in.

The page turns and someone whispers the story. It

seems there was this man who fell foul of the Gods. I couldn't quite catch his name but that is unimportant; it is only a story.

One day he stopped by a lake and scooping mud from the bank he moulded the clay into the most exquisite woman. As she reclined and warmed in the sun he lay on top of her and breathed life into her.

Their breaths were one, says the voice, and for a long time they breathed together within the kiss. When they made love they breathed apart, and afterwards she rose and walked away from the lake and her creator, and into the land of men.

The man was sad for a while at her leaving, but he got over it. There was still a lot of mud for moulding and he knew what he had to do.

The voice draws breath and turns another page. I drift in and out of the story which is often mumbled like a prayer. But it came to pass that the Gods were angry at what the man had done with the mud. It was a case of demarcation, they insisted. It was Gods who created, not man. And look what he had done: this most exquisite woman. And look what he had done to her, there, by the lake, brazenly in the open air. What would the neighbours think?

So they took this man, the voice tells me, and chained him to the top of the highest tower in the land. Then they summoned an eagle to circle and swoop and to perch upon the enchained man. The eagle's beak tore apart skin and flesh and feasted, there and then, upon the man's liver.

Well, the voice continues, he screamed and screamed and screamed, but the Gods refused to let him die. Each dawn he was alive, and each dawn the eagle came. So everybody knew, and everybody saw, and everybody heard and knew what they must not do.

I soar, I circle, I swoop. There is food below for my young. And as the air rushes by I see Dermot rushing up and I feel my feathers turn to skin. When I fall the pages flicker and the covers snap shut. I am awake, eyes open wide, and shivering.

The evening draws in. I have no young to fend for nor a lover to turn to, but life inches on. Inexorably. If there is no life after death then surely there is no death after life. Now is forever. As in 'do you take this man for ever and ever and ever?'

And did he take me? You bet.

And what did I get?

The static whirls on the radio as two people from different airports talk about a woman who had loved important men. She herself was so talented but that was beside the point, as were the important men. The point was that she had suffered. How she had suffered!

As a girl she had been in a terrible accident, a motor accident, and a long shaft of metal had speared her. The shaft pierced her womb and emerged from her body through her vagina. This meant, a voice whirled, that she could never have children. Never, forever.

I am sure that the thoughts of having children were far from her mind at that time, much less the thoughts of doing anything about it, with or without important men. But the thoughts did not remain far from her mind.

There would come a time, there would come a time when a child would not only be on her mind but in her body. What a miracle that must have been for a child to grow in there in that violated temple – but the voice swirls that she could never have children.

So, lest the Gods be angry, it must wither and die. But it did not actually wither, though it did die. No, it simply froze like a bloom in ice within its own embryo.

Scandalous woman that she was, she kept the thing. She did not care what the neighbours said but kept the foetal pearl in a sealed bell jar, there, floating in formaldehyde on the shelf inside her study. It was her first born and where one flower grew there would be others to follow. Oh, she knew all about eagles, and snakes; but she had pain enough not to care. This is my son, she would say, in whom I am well pleased.

But what have I, as evening turns to night and the shadows creep in? I have a kitchen that whirrs with dials that spin. Upon its spotless surfaces hotplates glow at the wave of my hand and cauldrons bubble. Behind what looks like a television screen a casserole froths and spits prime time beef for Dermot's TV dinner.

I am a witch at the centre of this technological cavern and I cackle as I dance with my broom. What would the neighbours think? What would they say? Enough, I think, to have poor Grace taken away. But away from what?

I remember the hospital doors and how they swung open with a push. And both with a circular window at head height, like two giant eyes, eyes that winked as they swung open wide.

I pushed through in some trolley or chair, I don't really remember; but Dermot was there, somewhere. Yes, he was there because I remember how he insisted that I give him the vessel.

Oh, it is all returning and it is all so clear; if only

someone would turn on the lights. Or is this just one dream that I never wrote down?

It was a large vessel of indiscernible shape, cold to the touch and cradled on my lap. Although it was cold and heavy, I did not want to relinquish it, being all that I carried by way of luggage. A liquid slopped about inside of it, something so vile that I dare not look. Or perhaps so exquisitely beautiful.

After all, what had Lot's wife seen? Or was it just that she had been told not to look – and disobeyed? I see her naked and silent, intricately carved in salt and smiling, knowingly. But I would not look and could not relinquish it.

There was something of a struggle. Dermot's manicured hands trying, with surprising strength, to wrestle it from me. I recall biting his hairy wrist, just above his snakeskin watchstrap, and gaining short advantage in the sharp yelp that followed. But more hands came, out from the shadows.

I knew the shapes and I knew the danger, I had seen it all beneath the gothic cathedral. I knew that if you wanted something badly enough you can make it yours, if you have the strength. They wanted that part of me badly enough to make it theirs – they had strength in numbers. And Dermot was a part of them and they a part of him; I could hear the same slithering and soothing sounds from each. I knew where they lived – never never land.

Night falls all over the city. Rain hisses persistently beneath the chattering of the cicadas. An owl throws a question out into the darkness. The only lights I see as I look over the rooftops are the million blue flickerings of television screens like a cheap pastiche of the firmament.

The Falling Dream

I lift up my eyes and there is nothing, but I rise to meet it anyway. And each pinpoint of rain becomes a star and I am impaled upon their points. I soar, I circle, I swoop, while below in toytown, in never never land, blank eyes turn into television screens while their bodies turn into shadows. I am above all that, falling toward the centre of the swirling galaxy, falling, falling, falling...

It was the falling dream awoke me. I was being peculiar again. I search for the pen and paper I keep handy so I can write down the important bits. On the bedside table a cup of cold coffee lies. Through a chink in the curtains the sun shines, and as I squint my eyes I see a thin sliver of cloud pass across it. My old friend, the falling dream.

Still Life with Seaweed

BRADY wished that he was somewhere else. In the oily sweat of Mulligan's Bar perhaps, amidst student banter and journalistic backslapping, the querulous whine of busmen wafting like music to the snug where he would sit – a folded newspaperman in the corner. In Philadelphia perhaps, but not here; enduring and not enjoying Art in the capital, and with a capital A.

Before him, under the gimlet glare of approximately thirty pairs of glazed eyes, on a makeshift stage beneath a web of hanging fishing nets a corpulent Englishman reclined, bollock naked, on a stagnant heap of seaweed. Gesturing limpidly with one hand, in the other he held a remote control gizmo with which he conducted a slide show of his apparently tedious life; he droned a quasi-poetic commentary for each banality that he summoned onto the screen.

Typically and pathetically Rawlins, thought Brady, and knowing this artist to be humourless to a fault could discount the merest notion that the performance might intend sending up its audience. Brady mentally lampooned it and allowed to enter the scene a laconic and large-boned broadcaster who, advancing on the rancid charade with a red volume tucked beneath his arm, announced: Trevor Rawlins, artist, poet, sage; arsehole of the highest water – this is your life!

Brady stifled a titter at his private joke, forcing bubbles to the surface of his white wine. Beside him the young woman in the tight fitting woollen cardigan and hippy hat touched his arm and murmured; "Poetic, isn't it?"

43

The Benefits of Tobacco

He couldn't be bothered looking for irony and there were now a myriad bubbles, his wine glass like a water cooler in an opium den. Sorcha was her name, 'Scorcher' to the long tongued wolves who comprised her louche coterie – for she had an Art College reputation, which Brady knew vaguely, for talent and outrage. But it was not really those two things which had caught Brady's eye.

If he had been elsewhere, in the aforementioned Mulligan's for instance, he would have engaged one of his folded companions in the customary intellectual repartee along the lines of: "Now, that woman in the hat has damn poor taste, but a fine pair of tits."

And one of them might wonder, just wonder if she might be willing: "For a world wide exclusive, a kiss and tell, an expose; do you think she would be willing to sail the sausage up the Liffey? Do you think she could make her monkey smile for the bald sentry?"

In truth, Brady was too cultured to hold with such coarseness, or at least to outwardly express it. No; but she did have a fine pair of tits. It was the manner in which the slight woollen material stretched over the cantilevered thrust of her brassiere that was so remarkable. How many years had the cream of Scottish engineering devoted to the achievement of that gravity-defying lift, that breathtaking separation? Brady's designer mind mused with approval.

Poetic – isn't it?

"Very," he said and struggled to apply himself to less base, if less interesting, considerations. To that which exalted the mind, the soul, nay the very grit and essence of the universe: Art. So, with a Liebfraumilch in one hand and a Pre-Raphaelite girl on the other, Brady turned to regard the stage below where, at that very precise moment,

Still Life with Seaweed

Trevor Rawlins was rapidly approaching puberty.

There was a review to be written and he was guiltily aware that, in the cold light of day, he would again cull from the dreary and redundant lexicon of art criticism the two hundred odd words that would satisfy his pretentious editor, confound the general reader and annoy no-one in particular. The word 'juxtaposition' leapt from Rawlins' turgid monologue and behind Brady a partition crashed to the floor.

A student, a gatecrasher, squeezed through the breach and took up an unsteady position beside Brady. Thirty pairs of eyes turned and looked down through thirty pairs of nostrils before, growing bored, they looked away again. Brady imagined that he was perhaps alone in thinking this was not part of the performance – its effect being more surprisingly real than anything Rawlins had hitherto achieved. Though, at the same time, he could not imagine why, in the name of God, anyone would want to gatecrash this of all parties.

The student gazed wildly about, a full-faced young countryman with three days stubble and a full tank of gas in his belly – in a word 'drunk'. How did Brady know he was a student? A book by Dostoevsky bulged the pocket of his hacking jacket, his lapel badge boasted the obscure legend 'Cosey Fanni Tutti', he wore a striped scarf; and all of the foregoing personal description. Anyway, you just knew these things.

The student gazed wildly about. "Where's the wine?" he said, condensing the sentence, after the German fashion, into one barely decipherable word.

"None left." said Brady who was nearest and wished to be both helpful and abrupt.

The Benefits of Tobacco

"Blue Nun? Just the ticket." and he smacked his lips, loudly.

"Sshhh!" said a Serious Person.

"Hush yourself. Hey, how ya doin', gorgeous..."

"Go away." said Sorcha, and turned her back on him.

"Don't I know you...without your clothes on?" the young man drawled as he oozed past Brady to take a perch by that smouldering cold shoulder. His right hand dropped from sight and Sorcha hopped suddenly, like burnt bread in a toaster.

"Fuck off." she told him, with low caste feeling.

"Sshhh!" said the Serious Person again, spraying Brady's face with atomised cheap wine. But Brady, being our main protagonist, had decided on more decisive action and gripped the student by the arm.

The young man, so roughly handled, was suitably outraged; "What's the meaning of this?" he demanded, loudly enough to be heard by Rawlins who was visibly irritated by the insinuation – as if it mattered.

"I haven't a clue." hissed Brady, "But you're either gone or mincemeat."

The sound of further mayhem told Brady that there were student reinforcements in the breach, beersmelling, boisterous and eager to enjoin battle. Distracted he loosed his grip and looked around, but immediately a strong arm looped his neck and the tables were turned.

"Fergal!" and "Conor!" and "Yahoo!" shouted the intruders.

"Got you now – submit!" roared the first student.

"Sshhh, sshhh, sshhh!." went the Serious Person encouraged now by friends as he hopped and hissed like a boiler about to blow. It was then that Brady's eardrum was rent by a scream as his assailant collapsed and was swallowed up by the football terrace surge of artwatchers and gatecrashers. A phalanx of men in dress suits and droopy moustaches arrived, heavily upholstered and ugly penguins who wrestled the intruders and, quite unfairly, the Serious Person.

Brady, released, was spun into a reel which brought him back into contact with Sorcha, softly bouncing to rest off her tender extremities. Triumphantly she waved a vicious looking hat pin before his eyes.

"Say thanks. I nearly had that bastard's balls on a kebab."

Brady was not one given to praise, winced in fact with a vicarious stab of pain.

"Let's get the hell out of here." he said, as the melee of giant penguins, students and disgruntled art-lovers wheeled towards them like a drunken and voracious octopus.

"But it's just getting interesting." she protested.

God, he hated that word, 'interesting', as in anything beyond comprehension, as in every college tutor cop-out when confronted by the hopeless attempts of some inept student. But he doubted that she meant it like that; interesting, from her it was an invitation.

"It's just ending." he said, but with some faint hope that a beautiful relationship was just beginning.

Deftly picking his space, our hero guided Sorcha out through the gutted partition and, glancing back, he even managed to feel a little bit sorry for Trevor Rawlins. There stood the artist on a midden in a wrecked room with a violent hokey-pokey encircling him, his pathetic sex swinging beneath his pendulous gut, arms outstretched in

The Benefits of Tobacco

a vain attempt to give girth to his shrill, girlish voice:

"Ladies and gentlemen please ... try and show a little decorum..."

See Emily Play

I STAND on the headland looking down at the town below, the sea is away to my left and the harbour ahead and to my right. The sun is sinking, swollen, into the hills and the gulls wheel and cry about the cliffs beneath me. That's the complete picture, I can put in the details later. Picture is appropriate, that is the way I see things, through a lens framed by a rectangle. The camera whirrs as I take another, and another, and another, swivelling slowly until I have it all in three hundred and sixty degrees. Are all photographs true? Does the camera ever lie? It is a question of timing, I believe, or time, you only last so long in a photograph, you really need to be there.

The last stop on my panorama is the camp site, the posh end where the big mobile homes rest. Is there anything more desolate, more heartbreaking than a caravan park at dusk, the night before the holiday season? Anything more pregnant with promise?

The night before the holiday season I would usually sit alone in my caravan, shuffling photographs of my past. I would take a bottle of wine onto the patio and drink till the sun went down. Then I would drink some more. This time I was going to stay and see it. This time I wasn't going to rent the thing out.

Each year is always going to be different. We all tell ourselves that. That's why I was staying on this year, usually I only used the place in June and September, I rented it on holiday weekends and throughout July and August. Something made me stay, I could smell life starting up again. I hoped I was right.

The Benefits of Tobacco

I suppose it was going to be different for Emily too. I had seen the kid before, pleasantly fair, supple, a good kid you would think from watching her, they were mostly good kids. It really did turn out different for Emily, for us all.

A small town nestles in the cove. There are several pubs of varying quality, a half dozen eateries mostly of the fish and chip variety, a battered cinema, two smallish supermarkets and amongst the few B&Bs, one good hotel. On each end of the cove are rival amusement arcades, and on waste ground near the harbour there is a carnival at high season.

There is much more to the town than the above, of course, but the above is what I wrote, more or less, in describing the town for the travel guide which I sell some work to. They use one of the photographs I have taken also, a not very flattering one. I wonder do my efforts keep the foreign tourists away. Probably not. There are more each year and the town is losing some of that neglected quality which I love so well, so selfishly well. A couple of years ago they were saying that the town was dying, the old Grand Hotel had closed and the picturesque Marine Hotel burned down, suspiciously. People's habits had changed, they wanted sun and sex, and they got little of it here, little of the sun anyway. They were wrong, of course, but they will be right someday, inevitably they will be right about forthcoming death.

I have known them for years, the locals, and they have known me, there are even some with whom I am on first name terms, but only a few. They don't know what I do, no, they don't know they have a spy in their midst. They see me with my prying eye and they don't even guess, they haven't a clue, not a dickeybird.

See Emily Play

In the morning, the first morning of my summer holidays – hah, that's a good one! In the morning I manage to open one eye, my squinting eye, and note that the weather is reassuringly normal. A dull grey fog envelops everything and anything more than twenty feet away is well nigh invisible. I get dressed, have a smoke and make for the town. I know where it is.

It is a twenty minute walk if I take the laneway through the fields, joining the main road into town right beside the one good hotel. Along the laneway I hear sheep bleating and scattering mingled with a naggingly familiar sound, a rasping, tingling sound. A human voice shouts and fades into the distance. But there are no stories for me in a mist, I need clear air.

I stop in the first coffee shop in the town, the Coffee Deck, such a habit of mine that I am well known there. Rachel, with her lovely green eyes and plump innocent face, greets me by name. More lovely each year, I think, less plump and less innocent too.

"So, how have you been keeping?" she begins, and we settle into familiar conversations, update ourselves on the activities of names we know. I tell her about my disintegrating family, I tell her my problems.

"Maybe things will work out," she says, "and you might see things much clearer, down here, away from it all."

I point out that the mist has, so far, stopped me from seeing anything at all.

"When it lifts, then." she says, and I realise that it was never what Rachel said that mattered so much as the way she said it. It is that beautiful musical lilt that seems to squash all pessimism. When it lifts, then, and I repeat that phrase in my own flat monotone:

"When it lifts."

The Benefits of Tobacco

I am distracted as I see Emily and some friends ghost past the window, I feel a sudden, strange, lurch in my stomach and am torn, inexplicably, between a desire for her to come in and some unnamed dread that she will do so. Rachel, who has been talking about photography, is suddenly snapping her fingers before my eyes.

"Oy! Anyone home?"

She follows my eyes and grimaces, not seeing anything there, everything swallowed by the mist. I apologise and listen again to her news and her plans. I should pay closer attention to such things, if not for a friend then for myself, after all, I could use the money.

There is a canon pointing out to sea. That is a little joke; there are two, I am sitting on the cannon and pointing my Canon out to sea. "Bejesus, it's Cher shooting a new video." I turn to see my favourite culchie advancing towards me off the dock. Sean Dwyer, local auctioneer, his hands in his pockets and the flap of his blazer fluttering behind him. Sean really does have a red neck, and even though he is a former inter-county footballer and built like a prop-forward, I can get away with ribbing him about it.

I get some work off Sean, not a lot, dribs and drabs, but it's work and we'll usually seal the deal with a mother of all drinking bouts. We get on.

"Fucking Jackeens. Won't believe it unless you photograph it."

"I thought that was Yanks." I point the camera at him to annoy him.

"Please! Unless you want to deliver it later at St Mary's." St. Mary's being the local maternity hospital.

We chew the fat, he knows my situation and skirts around it; his wife, Jean, and mine are friends. It all goes way back. He's planning an expedition out to the islands, a spot of fishing – and asks me to come along.

"You'll love it. And if you start going on about art we can maroon you on Seal Island!"

"What, again?" This is true, they did that once although I think it was a genuine error – they simply forgot that I had been with them. I accept.

"You just behave." says Sean and smiles. He changes tack abruptly, "Have you seen my gobshite son?"

"Brian?" Sean has two boys and Colm, the eldest, has just started university.

"Ay, Brian." says Sean, and with a resigned, vaguely defeated shrug, turns and walks briskly away. "If you see him, send him home." he shouts over his shoulder, and is gone. I wonder about Brian for a moment, some people make you wonder.

Last year was our last family holiday, last year we all played happy families here at the beach. The White Strand, treacherous at full tide with the river flowing in to the south, is best at low tide with its wide expanse of beach uncovered and the rock pools below the cliffs facing north. On the second day I am there already, reliving it all. I see Sile walk the kids, Lena and Barry, towards the pounding surf, I feel the sun on my skin, I turn another page of the book. There is somebody watching me.

There is nobody watching me now. There are few here, around the corner of the cliffs is the cove where the people go to watch the dolphin play. Here, today, on the second day, there is a couple up on the rocks, sunning themselves in the faint sun. She is stripped to the waist and he, long-haired and fat, is naked. It is distracting, they are so oblivious of everything and I am so aware of them. They weren't there last year, you didn't do that sort of thing last year; but there is no point thinking about that – I know that I cannot go back there.

Someone is watching me. I remember turning that page and... two girls are walking the sandy path down from the fields. Mid teens in one piece swimsuits, one carries a shortened surf board. It is Emily, and she floats past without even a sideways glance.

When Lena and Barry returned, breathless, they were full of garbled excitement about the surf board.

"Lady let us use her surfboard." Barry gasped.

Lena was older and not so easily impressed; "She was no lady." she scoffed.

Sile and I had a good laugh at that, much to Lena's disgust. "I meant she was only a girl," she insisted. I think it's what I miss most, really, the laughing at nothing, the private jokes. Oh, I miss the warmth at night, I do, I miss that too.

The sun comes out on the second day. My hangover is not nearly so bad, although there is a curious taste in my mouth. I hear the shouts and the sheep, again. What is going on out there? There are holes in my memory. I remember it took me ages getting to sleep, the bigger kids were playing for ever in the playground, for ever and ever. I hope I hadn't done anything foolish, like telling them to fuck off, but there is a vague and immature recollection of giggling and footsteps in the dark. What of it!

At the Coffee Deck Rachel asks me to the dance. Just like that. She's talking to a couple of local youths and she shouts over to me: "Oy, Neil, are you coming to the dance on Saturday?"

Me? I was miles away and a bit embarrassed to see the three white faces turn to me. I hummed and hawed.

"Ah, forget it." she said. The boys smirked.

One of the boys was Brian, Sean's son. I remember then that he had been hanging around the playground at the site. I remembered his voice and I remembered the name he called. That was the name and the laughter that echoed through my sleep.

I am of that age where I begin to consider the merit of such cliches that youth is wasted on the young. I suppose so much of it was wasted on me. Wrapped in such gloomy thoughts I have a solitary pint at Moriarty's and walk back towards the site. Rachel hails me from the Coffee Deck. She's all business now, talking about the photographs I had apparently agreed to do for the refurbishment.

The refurbishment? Rachel is taking over the Deck, as it will be called, she is, she says, going to be a mover and a shaker. I can well believe it. The earlier business seems forgotten until I turn to leave.

"You know your problem?" she says, "You think you're too old, but you've never really grown up."

"Eh?"

"The dance. You're afraid to go in case people look at you and say: ah, the oldest swinger in town."

"I'm not afraid..."

"You're afraid, like a boy would be afraid. You've got to take your place in the world..."

"Act like a man?"

"Just be yourself."

"Jesus, I'll go to the bloody dance if you want..."

"You don't have to go if you don't want to."

"I'll go!"

With that Rachel was suddenly satisfied and set about her dusting and polishing, the mid-day sun having burned off the customers. I left, red-faced, unsure whether that constituted a date or a challenge. What an odd woman, I thought, what a strange girl.

That evening I take my glass of wine, I take my beaker of wine, over to the perimeter fence where there is a good view of the sea and the lights of the town below. Up to my left the green sward is glowing, melting down over the cliffs. The folly on top looks majestic, dramatic against the cerulean sky. I consider strolling up there and taking a time exposure.

So I find myself as evening falls climbing along the green edge of the cliffs towards the ancient folly. Gulls are wheeling and away to the right, where I dare to peep over the precipice I see they have white streaked the cliffs around their cacophonous city. I have to lie on my belly to look over the edge and as I do the roll I have taken today slips from my breast pocket and slithers over the side. It bounces down the steep slope towards the very edge where it lodges on a stone. Well, fuck it anyway. A brave man would go and retrieve his property, it had taken me all day to get those shots: ay, a foolish man would risk his life for a day's work. I could take them again. So the light would be different and the details would never be the same, but the details never are.

Worse and worse again was the fact that I had sneaked some pictures of Emily. Sneak is not really the word; herself and Brian were hanging around together down at the boardwalk, near the dolphin trips, and I went and asked them, actually asked them, would they mind. They didn't, in fact they were naturals, as young lovers are; at least Emily, tanned and Titian haired, seemed a natural to me. So sneak isn't the word. Fuck it anyway.

Again I hear the sheep and the shouts, and the harsh rasp of something metallic. Distracted, a bit irritated, I turn onto my side to look up towards where the noise is coming from. I see the sheep scattering over the hillside and behind them, cutting through them now, a stiff figure on a bike, whooping and ringing his raspy bell. There is something amusing about the scene and my curiosity draws me towards it. I forget about the film and head towards the ditch. The man on the bike has reached the bottom of the field and turns around to push his bike up the hill again. I walk parallel to him and hail him at the top.

He looks a sprightly fifty something, a shock of iron grey hair and creased features giving him a passing resemblance to Samuel Beckett. I had taken him to be a local, since the place is flush with eccentrics, but his accent is foreign, Australian or maybe South African. There is something about his wild eyes that convey a sense of religious fervour. I tell him he could herd better with a dog.

He laughs. "I'm not herding, I'm chasing."

"Why chase sheep?"

He shrugs, "Because they're there." It's my turn to laugh. We exchange cigarettes and chat easily for a while. He has been living here for almost a year, an oasis of sanity in a mad, mad world is his explanation. There is a past buried in there, something he's not going to tell me so I don't ask.

"I see you take photographs." he says.

"Don't all tourists?"

"Are you a tourist?" It wasn't really a question and I can only shrug, non-commitedly, in reply. He hoists up his bike again, with mock weariness, and returns to his sport. "I think they quite like it really." he says, and heads off down the hill again.

The Benefits of Tobacco

I call into Sean the next day to see if he has any small premises to let. If I'm going to stay here for the summer I will need a decent darkroom, hell, even an indecent darkroom. Sean is more interested in the fishing expedition.

"Can you bestir yourself tomorrow and pick us up some bait, the other lads are busy and I'm..."

I am prepared for this and have a litany of cast iron excuses prepared.

"Y'know," says Sean, "You'd be better off going down to the chipper and getting a battered cod and chips. And you can puke up after it instead of before it as you'll be doing tomorrow, because you're fuck all use in a boat."

I was telling him about the roll of film when Brian dropped in. He had Emily in tow, and she stood sullen guard by the door. I gave her the most imperceptible of nods and she replied in kind. If she was following this lanky streak of misery who was now panning for his father's gold then she did it with a suitable air of diffidence; yet I had sensed in Emily over the last few days that sense of desperation, that over eager flaunting of herself that spoke as much of needs and wants as it did of desire.

"Ah, you gobshite." Sean said as he turned to his son, then laughed when he saw Brian's face drop. "I'm talking to him, to Neil. Dropped his roll of film over the cliff at the folly. Stuck there, just above the drop. Bejesus, just as well it wasn't a wedding roll, you'd be winching it up by helicopter."

"I'll get them for you, if you like," Brian said, he had a surprisingly meek voice for his loutish appearance.

"You, mister," said Sean, "Can keep away from those cliffs, if I hear..."

Brian switched on his look of teenage disdain and Sean relented, shoving a note at him, "Here's a fecking tenner, now don't spend it on anything that smells."

My eyes were drawn reluctantly back to Emily. She was staring at me with deep ambiguity. If you want it, that look seemed to say, get it yourself. Whatever it is, get it yourself.

I wasn't the oldest at the dance, not by a long chalk. Sean was there holding up the bar. Apparently it was the best known late extension in the county, the things you miss when you have young kids! So, for the first time in eight years visiting the town I put my elbow into a pool of beer and ordered a pint without even thinking of losing my glass slipper in the rush home.

"Where the fuck were you, today?"

"I didn't think you needed me."

"Jesus, you're terrible fucking sensitive all the same."

I asked them did they catch anything at about the same time that the band started up again and I caught precious little of the subsequent yarn, nothing but the odd spray of spittle, several expletives and a few references to his 'gobshite son' who apparently was filling my spot in the boat. By the end of the tale I was scanning the perimeter of the floor for signs of... I wasn't too sure, actually, who.

Rachel rescued me later, stealing up behind me and poking me in the ribs. She was radiant or maybe drunk, probably both, and was trailing a rat-faced youth, swigging from a bottle, who seemed about to go for your throat each time he spoke. Rachel after an age of screaming in my ear, eventually got me onto the dance floor and we left the rat in the increasingly maudlin company of Sean.

I see his drowning eyes follow me onto the floor but I

don't dwell on that. As I fold into Rachel's embrace I think how pleasantly she cushions our collision and yet, yet how small and fragile are her shoulders, her back. I am enjoying myself at last. I married too young, I really did, and surrendered too soon to the unique solitude of responsibility. Oh, all the things I had been missing.

We float past the bar again and I see Sean's eyes unglaze and look towards me with sudden precision. But it is not at me that he is looking, we have bumped against Brian and Emily, and I see Brian's eyes looking defiantly back at his father, and I see Emily's eyes cast upwards in adoration, but not quite adoration.

The dance ends and we spill with everyone out into the garish light of the carpark. Suddenly it occurs to me that I have no place to go, there is no place like home and there is no place to go to. I look at Rachel and see how much she belongs here, as much a part of the town as the mountains and the harbour and the amusements; the tides that have washed over her and retreated back to sea, the comings and goings of the dolphin; she might come and go herself – but this will always be her place.

There is a chip van where we dally before giving up. We are stuck for a while with the rat-faced youth and his catch of the night in a round of joke telling and cigarette swapping that passes off well enough before finding ourselves alone. Alone on the high road leading up towards the site.

It gets to the point that Rachel is standing closer than she should and for a giddy moment, no, longer than that really, I feel that I should fuck her, that the two of us should fuck like minks somewhere in the feral undergrowth. And I feel, in so much as I can ever be confident in predicting such things, that the chances of it coming to pass is in fact better than fifty-fifty, is closer to ninety or ninety five per cent. So, I could find myself in a field, or in a stony cove, heavily exploring those parts of Rachel about which I may previously have idly speculated, and that I would screw her rigid not once but several times before the cock crowed. And then, and then...?

When it all came to pass, it never happened at all. We watched the moon evaporate above the deepest and calmest of seas, finished off the sixpack, cracking open the tops with her sharp teeth, smoking ourselves to ecstatic and isolated death. Tomorrow, we said when we parted, tomorrow.

There are two paths back to the site, the high road as I have mentioned, and a low path, a dirt track that skirts the bay and is favoured by fishermen, and young lovers.

On the high road there is a particularly scenic vantage point overlooking the bay, the town below and the mountainous far shore. Tonight under a full moon, with the moonlight and streetlight flickering in unison in the dewy early Summer air, it is achingly beautiful. I lean on the wall there and smoke my last cigarette. My eyes are focussed on the low path. Just there where it bends around the rocks a couple embrace, oblivious to the fact that they are highlighted by the one streetlamp on that dark stretch of road. Perhaps oblivious. It is Emily and Brian. What are they doing? What is she going to do for him? I wonder if, looking out at the world over his shoulder, if she can see the match flare in my cupped hands and cast a menacing shadow across my face.

In that uneasy sleep my dreams are haunted by ghosts, my body struggles against drowning in the swollen sheets.

The Benefits of Tobacco

I am so alone out here, so desperately alone, yet when dawn steals in to take another night from me I sense a figure cold and impassive, loom above the bed. Blearily I look up towards the misty face and it leans down to me. It is the face of some poor wretch, a beggar or a thief, the expression frozen in a mirthless gurn that it has fooled itself into believing is a smile. But there is something awful that I recognise in there, those thin lips and hooded eyes, the hot, supercilious stare; I see my father dying and I close my eyes again. I feel its breath on my cheek, the stench of old alcohol and spicy meat, the voice is nasal and rasping, oh, I have heard that voice before.

"You are afraid." it says.

"Of what?" I ask, "Of death?"

"No, not death. Death is easy. You get used to death and there is so little to do."

"Who are you?" I ask, getting colder and colder.

"I am the reason you are afraid." it says, the voice mercifully getting weaker, pulling the cold off somewhere with it. "I am you. Yes, if you opened your eyes you'd see, I am you."

A drunken cackle echoes around the van and as it grows fainter I manage to sneak my eyes open, but there is nothing there. I chew on the vile gum of sleep, parched and empty, if only I could have tasted Rachel's kisses or captured the merest hint of her perfume. But there is nothing there, and no place to go but home.

One last time I mount the hill towards the folly, so apt that, so apt; and from that vantage point the town will be so small that I can hold it in the palm of my hand. What more disasters can I prevail upon its inhabitants, what more love can I lavish on them, or on some of them, never to have it understood, never to have it truly requited. It is said that amongst primitive peoples there is a great suspicion, a superstition regarding photography; they are convinced that the photograph captures more than the image and that it captures the soul as well. They know this not through knowledge of the process but through intuition; how wise they are to put their trust in that!

I climb the hill one last time and hear the bleating of the sheep and shouts, the music of the spokes and rasping bells. Over to my right a slight figure is perched precariously on the cliff's edge and I notice flowers have been strewn underfoot, but I cannot linger now. I reach the top of the hill in time to see the man, the priest, I suppose, complete his first run and turn to push his bike up to the summit again.

I rise to meet him when he comes close, but while he is friendly, happy even, I have noticed something weary in his step.

"A fine day." I say.

"Ay, thanks be to God." he answers, with a practised local nuance. He turns those steel blue eyes out to sea.

The dolphin is jumping in the bay, boy is that dolphin up for it. "It's well for some." I say.

He thinks a moment with his face still turned from me. You've seen that profile before, from out of the darkness as the hatch slides back, it knows your secrets, or thinks it does.

"They say that the dolphin has found a lover." he says, "And that he is going to follow her out to sea."

"The town will miss him, he'll take a lot of the trade with him."

The priest thinks a moment and turns to look into my

eyes; "But he will be back amongst his own."

Our eyes turn now to the figure on the cliff, I recognise her and remark how dangerous it is there, just as Sile would have, had she been here. "A wind could come and..."

"But it has. Haven't you heard?"

I make my way back towards the site in some confusion. I come to where Emily waits at the spot where I had dropped my roll on Friday. She walks towards me without any apparent recognition, she clutches a homemade wooden cross to her chest.

"A boy died here last night." she says. "But I can't get this cross into the ground."

She holds out a crumpled piece of paper to me, it has been torn from a newspaper and is part of a photograph of a schoolboy football team hoisting the cup of victory. I know that photograph, it hangs on the wall of Sean Dwyer's office.

"This is the boy?"

She nods; "It's the only photograph I have." She looks back towards the cliff edge and passes the cross, almost offhandedly, to me. Emily has made some attempt to point the butt of the cross but the ground is hard and it doesn't penetrate easily.

For days I could see the impression it left on my palms but at least I got it to stand in the earth, and that was what she wanted. She thanked me and I left her there, there was nothing more to do.

I did not go to the funeral. Nothing remained. The next morning, very early, I packed up and left, drove out along the only road and kept on driving as it widened and widened, I was taking the river home from its source unto the sea. I never looked back, I never went back, I only went home.

Some years later I saw the ex-priest on television. I was right, he had been a priest. He talked about faith and redemption. He talked about his experiences in the town. He even talked about God. He told us that the dolphin had found a mate, the dolphin had found a mate and had wandered back to sea. All things come to an end, all things come to pass. I know I will always remember my years in the town and the leaving of it, but I really don't think about it all that often.

Pushing the River

I CAN hear her whisper in the hiss of the machine, see the imprint of her face on the darkened screen, she just won't go away – will she? I suppose some people never know when to quit. I can type her name now, call her up; this new technology makes it all so easy, you need barely move your fingers, just think of it. Just think. There, exactly where I knew that it would be ... Sorcha.

Sorcha. It is all about her, and what I became. And what I have become is little more than a teller of tales. I blink my eye and wonder if anything will come and fill this space. It usually does.

There is always love, I suppose ... yes, go on, love and death ... yes, and? There is always love and death because they come to us all even if we have never asked. Love and death ... and? go on ... I will call it: Love, Death and the Lady. Because, because it all begins with love, and ends, as it inevitably does, with death. Because, like everything, I have heard it somewhere before; love, death and the lady. But she was no lady.

This is really the end, the very end. All that remains is a charred and crumpled photograph, the sense of loss from exaltation not enjoyed; oh, and all the words that are to follow. Why should I care? It didn't really happen to me and what happened would probably not amount to much if left uninflamed by my imagination. And who cares about that?

Alison cares. One morning she awakes and she sees long clawmarks running diagonally down my back. I feel the fury in the silence as my eyes unstick; that space between us where Tara must insert herself each morning yawns to an unbridgeable gap. Then Alison runs a finger along one red weal:

"What was she like?"

"A lioness," I breathe, "a wild animal."

But they were not the words for such situations. They may be true but there are other words. There is the truth and there is nothing. Silence. Nothing but the truth, but never the whole truth.

A neon sign hums against the rain. It flashes, intermittently, without the certainty which flashing signs should display. The sign says sweet fuck all, but that is just a joke. No bad way to begin, standing in torrential rain before an ominously failing joke.

One window glows with yellow light. Otherwise the smalltown street is grey, deserted. Someone is working late. That would be me.

Above the town the headland is thrust like a defiant fist into the sea; its great knuckles of granite gaunt against the sky, its thin skin of soil stretched thinner from the constant clenching. It is as though in the palm of the fist lies some secret to be forever concealed from the snooping town. From the world. The elements seek to be a part of this conspiracy; the wind whipping foam from the wavetops into towering veils of vapour which it drapes around the headland like a spider wrapping its prey.

But the one window glows with yellow light and that is me. And I am not alone.

She is yellow skinned and she is naked. She sits on a storm tossed bed; her arms, stretched behind her for support, thrust her boyish torso forward. Her pubic hair is barely suggested in the shadow and slightly obscured by her long leading leg. Her nipples are very dark, almost black.

I take the scalpel and hold it, poised, at that tender area just to the front of her armpit. I pause. That is an area I like. It may not be erogenous, but it is erotic. At least to me – so there must be others who find it so. It is nicely picked out with a subtle highlight and I feel that I shouldn't change it for the world. But the nipples are too dark, if not for me then perhaps for Sam; so change it I must.

With the scalpel I cut from that tender spot and inscribe a perfect and steady arc beneath her left breast coming to a pinpoint stop at her breastbone. I peel the transparent skin back and leave her breast exposed. Yes, her nipple contrasts far too much with her tawny skin and anyway the breast is really too flat. Boyish. I must blow the frost of a highlight on there, and then touch up her nipple. Plastic surgery of a type, I suppose – but is it Art?

And is Art Truth?

But it is not the truth which concerns us here. After all, why bother spinning a yarn if it is to be spoiled in the end (worse, at the beginning) by appearing to be true. If we were so concerned with truth we would perhaps be better studying law, or history or the racing form on the turf accountant's wall.

I prefer to be naive. That way I can believe things which are clearly not the truth, or which are destined to remain unproven. So, if I were to tell you something, confide in you this thing that is troubling me, you would not be under any onus to believe it; I will do the believing for you.

The Benefits of Tobacco

Look on me as the person on the outside looking in, standing in my old macintosh in the rain while the joke sign hums and tells me sweet fuck all. I can't catch everything that goes on. I find myself saying: this is not right, it didn't happen quite like that. But you could say that the story starts like this.

Above the town the volcano sleeps, and in its slumber it curls an arm protectively around a narrow lake. You could say that the lake nestles in its wooded armpit, because at the head of the valley the bare, heathered downs give way to forest and woodland. So long as the volcano remains dormant, the water shows ne'er a ripple, shows only the sky and trees in its placid mirror. It reflects everything of our world the better to conceal everything in its own. But don't think that this apparent nothingness means that it is not dangerous, oh no. If the volcano is denied the volcano's right to fight with fire, why then should it not use its cousin, water, to drown the enemy at the foot of the valley?

At this precise moment that I visualise it, it is the picture of peace. A doe comes to sip from the waters, big eyes softly nervous and her coat a camouflage of ochre and dappled sunlight. A young girl trots a pony along the bridle path, bouncing plumply on the saddle and a serene smile on her lips. Birds chatter easily in the birchwood and soft furry animals shuffle through the evergreens. One day a lion will roar by the water's edge, but that is still some way off, we will cross that bridge when we come to it.

The lake is not real, of course. Nothing ever is these days. It is an artificial lake conceived of by mere mortals and scooped from the side of the mountain by those combined banalities of muscle, metal and engineering. It was put there not long after the forest, which is not real either; it was thought, correctly, that one would compliment the other and make from the threatening barrenness a place of beauty. And it was thought that the deer might like it, as they didn't really belong there either, having been uprooted from their Japanese homeland some decades before, and perhaps they could be tricked into believing that the views of the volcano that peeked through chinks in the forest were somehow after Hokusai, and his hundred views of Fujiyama.

So it is that down here in Brigadoon, we labour in our ticky-tacky shops and houses beneath a make-believe lake balanced precariously on an undercover volcano. Only a dam holds all that water back, a fragile wall of mud and stones, and keeps it from rushing hungrily down the valley to the sea. Push the river, Sorcha says, break the dam!

It is after the flood and a stained, stamped-on bromide sticks to the linoleum floor. I peel it up and pray that it does not disintegrate. So I stand in the sun that falls through the shattered roof with Sorcha in my arms again. Of course, it is only an image, a print taken from that first photograph I had of her; that famous Studio Magazine spread where she reclines on the bed, her arms pushing back for support and those long slim legs lightly crossed. Her body is twisted subtly to hide her sex though her almost boyish chest shows bare below the fall of her hair. Hair also hides half her face, averted and much in shadow, but I can still discern that sfumato smile tease the corner of her lips.

I could be there at the foot of her bed taking that picture, as I often imagined myself. But photographs, I

71

suppose, had been our undoing, or overexposure perhaps – to put it delicately. Instead this would be the last I would see of Sorcha. Curious then that the end should prove little different from the beginning, only slightly paler.

So much for bright beginnings.

When I first met Sorcha it was at that dreadful exhibition opening. As the best things in life are free, or so Alison says, it was fitting that the best thing about the opening was the free wine, both in quality and quantity it made for an excellent antidote to the paintings. Sam was there and I recall seeing him with a half bottle of wine in one hand and the other firmly gripping the buttock of a young lady. But I would find out later that she was no lady, and that her name was Sorcha.

It was much later that she insinuated herself into the life of the studio. I could tell by Sam's glazed and droopy look the place she held in his heart and loins. But I had not guessed that it was so strong, so persistent; but then how could I guess when I had yet to be bitten by the bug? And how was I to know that Sam was mad?

The magazine was Sam's idea. Sam was full of ideas, full of an infectious enthusiasm for life. Most people would agree; when asked they admitted that, yes, Sam was full of it. Before the magazine came the business. With the business came the studio. At first the studio was empty, and having been of late a funeral parlour I suppose we should have been thankful for that. But it was empty and it was dark, and the spirit of Sam moved over the rising damp.

I tell a lie, it was not entirely empty. It was once a funeral parlour and some of the accoutrements of that ghoulish trade had been left scattered about the place, as though the previous tenants had left in something of a hurry. I wondered why, and then considered it best not to wonder. A rubber glove hung from a shelf, a plastic bath lay on the stone floor of the back lobby, a mop, stiff with unmentionable stains, slouched against the door to the toilet and there were gauze bandages, scissors and tweezers scattered carelessly about.

There was something else, an ominous reminder of our mortality. It came as a shock and ultimately became, like the flashing sign, something of a joke.

What I remember is Sam standing there, in that long, low ceilinged room which would become the main studio. It is unfurnished, with three walls in dour wood panelling and a blood red carpet underfoot. The fourth wall is mostly window and the hammered opaque glass converts the light to smoke. Light sits uneasily in the room, as though it would rather be somewhere else, and fails completely to fall on the mansize recess set midway in the long facing wall; once home to a graven idol, I presume.

I remember Sam standing there, his arms raised in benediction. He is transported within, translucent – he is in fact transparent, something I should have noticed. He is a biblical looking man in a double breasted suit; red turning to grey at the split ends of his leonine mane and a paintbrush beard that juts arrogantly forward. Setting his arms akimbo and arching his back, he grins his brown-tooth grin at the ceiling and blesses the office with the madness in his eyes.

"Perfect, absolutely bloody perfect."

"Blood red perfect." I point out.

"Of course the carpet will have to go."

"Either the carpet goes or I go."

"No," he says, "On second thoughts we'll keep it. It has

73

that certain sleazy quality I'm looking for. The seamy underbelly of design and art, just perfect for the magazine."

Well, I laughed at that, but my laughter was always a weak mirror image of his.

"In here in the dark," he continues, "Just an angle lamp on. The floor a pulsating red and you leaning back on the swivel chair and looking out the clear window – that lemon shit glass has to go – and what do you see?"

I saw a bad case of enterprise fever, quite common in the graphics business. Sam had spent a long time in the graphics business climbing from the ad agency office brat to art director. Once famed as Leeson Street's lunchtime lounge lizard it had then gone terribly wrong. Some people say that Sam was found out, some say that he found God and sometimes I think that he found Art, with a capital A. Eventually he had found me in the bargain basement and swore that he would take the two of us up in that golden elevator bound for the top floor. We were going up! Can't you just feel it?

"A neon sign, very modern, we might even have Venetian blinds, thirtyish gumshoe stuff. The neon sign flashing our message to the world: Sam Fleming Associates – Design and Advertising."

Even then, when I was so innocent, I recall my mind muttering. Even then I projected that Sam Fleming Associates could be contracted to SFA, or sweet fuck all. Later, when he had calmed down a little, when we had paid a small fortune to have the sign made, I told him the joke. He laughed, of course, but the sign started flickering in that baleful way at that precise moment, and from that moment on.

Until the flood.

Sam was always prone to extremes and at first I thought that the other thing was one of his jokes. Then I noticed that it had taken the wind out of his sails, albeit very briefly.

"Who put this here? The fuck ..."

"Well," I quipped. "Every corpse has a purple lining."

He brightened. "Let this be a reminder to us, never miss a deadline." In the jerrybuilt extension at the back which might prove useful for sign work, the stench of death was palpable. There, laid on a trestle table, was an irregular hexagonal box: a pine coffin with polished brass handles and a vulgarly sumptuous cerise lining. Only the lid was missing, the lid and the corpse.

An unexpected recovery perhaps. Or some poor git ferried across the Styx in an orange crate instead. We never told anyone, not a soul, excepting those we knew most intimately. But we left it where we found it, I mean, you never know when something like that can come in handy.

Now, imagine what the studio became, moulded in the image of Sam's dream. It was half-tasteful in that the furnishings glinted appropriately with chrome and deep leather – at least it looked like leather at the time. The floor pulsated redness, cold fingers of air crept from the rere and tickled the back of my neck, the phones were *so* modern and the recess was left vacant in honour of the unknown deity that once lived there. Posters, calendars and bristleboard covered most of the panelling while a fish tank in the reception was never regarded as a portent of the coming flood. Towards the back of the building the darkroom door was ajar, inside the red pilot light of the Repromaster winked with technological cunning.

The Benefits of Tobacco

There, in the dark with only the anglepoise lamp on, I recline like a gumshoe and let my gaze escape through a slit in the blinds, up past the flickering sign to where a volcano rumbles above the town. That is, I sometimes think of it as a volcano and, in retrospect, with good reason.

I am not alone as I gaze, the gumshoe of graphics, out at the gathering storm. It is not just that I am with my painting, that prone and eager and malleable woman. The light is yellow and the page is yellow – but perhaps that is all to do with age, because it will all soon be over. And I can return to my warm bed and hear Alison growl safely in the dark, and Tara, my little cub, mewling softly in her place.

Sorcha is the other person there, lying back on the tossed sheets on the studio floor, her face in shadow and her body exposed. This is typical of her. She is trying to communicate platonic empathy but, very occasionally, she scratches her pubic triangle in a way that is distracting – to say the least. She must know by now that the graphic and glossy images I make from the poses she strikes are, more and more, taking on a greater than superficial resemblance to her. They are becoming her. They will outlast her. She wants that although she, yes even Sorcha, shudders at the thought of the use they will be put to in the meantime.

Sorcha had become the staple diet of the readers, if you could call them readers, of Studio Magazine. Whether provocative, pouting or pristine, she could always pose perfectly for the part; the camera loved her and the cameraman, Porno Pete, loved her. The readers of Studio loved her enough to masturbate over her image, Sam loved her to the point of openly groping her buttocks in company, and I loved her, furtively.

She would enter under the lamps, be photographed with various props, be trimmed and cropped and airbrushed, cut and pasted, processed, colour separated, etched, inked, rolled and pressed until she finally emerged as the lone lover's goddess to be bound, stapled, sold, scanned and thumbed; and maybe even poked in the eye.

That beckoning eye, set in the plastic realism of what I had made of her face. Her face. That was the enigma of this woman who presented her body so readily for the critical examination of a hidden audience; and for me within the intimacy of this room. Her face remained obscure. In all the photographs she held it so that shadow or hair or both fell protectively across it. Or she found dim places in a room, or kept the windows or the lamps behind her; there was even an aura about her that softened the definitions of her features. More than that there were her props, veils and wide brimmed hats and an endless supply of sunglasses. And, if ever I caught her in cold light, I would find her face painted exquisitely, the alabaster face of a woman of the floating world or the deathmask of an Egyptian queen.

Was she beautiful? That was something I had to learn. She had an anonymity to preserve in the face of publicity, and out of devotion to her mission in life, whatever that was. I now doubt that her apparent enthusiasm for the magazine was anything to do with that quest, it was simply a convenient focal point. It suited her purposes and, not having been summoned into existence at her whim, she made what use of it that she could. Anyway, neither she nor I had ever been taken in by the whole woolly ethos of the magazine as propounded by Sam.

Sam the philanthropist (very pissed at the time, in fact) had decided, he told me, that it would greatly benefit our much beleaguered artistic community if they had access to a professionally produced reference work for life drawing. It would also be a neat way of circumventing the censorship laws while plugging a gap in the soft porn market, practically creating the market in this country.

All truth is ultimately two dimensional. Truth's prison is the printed page, the finished painting. Only those images that are captured by the camera's lens or refracted through the artist's creative prism can be stored in Truth's top drawer. To fade, as only Truth fades, or to be found and used as evidence against you. That is all that remains, two-dimensional technical things; the rest is just a tissue of lies.

Exciting days were just around the corner, the machines were waiting there, crouched in the alleyways, smiling and seductive. And underneath the hard outer shell of the machines they wore soft undergarments. These were the dreams that money could buy.

I have studied long and hard, God knows I have, trying in my humanly imperfect way to perfect that small skill I possessed. Handcraft, hand-eye co-ordination, call it what you will, it is the grit that forms the pearl. I have studied, looked impassively into the eyes of the dead and those of the living, held and stroked cadavers, poked and kneaded human flesh. I have watched tears roll off my greased shoulder and marvelled at the reflections they held. I have paid my dues.

It was, in its own way, the pursuit of knowledge. But the machines just knew, smugly, certainly, and for a price they would tell you. What you see is what you get. And then everyone knew.

The centrepiece of a graphic design studio darkroom is a repro camera, a stat camera I believe the Americans call it. The top level, at about chest height, has a control panel and a hinged top that covers the glass carrier for the negative paper. The lens is fixed to the underside. A pulley system connects all this to the bottom level, the baseboard, which can descend almost to the ground. The baseboard is A2 size with a plate glass cover under which the designer places the artwork for reproduction. To each side is a powerful set of arc lamps. The developer is separate, a small unit kept adjacent to a sink. The whole system operates under a red safety lamp.

Sorcha had begun by lending me a book, and that is always a good sign. It is a gesture that compliments by taking you as one who reads, and it serves as an introduction to the lender's life. It is a form of long distance lovemaking – the first secret shared.

On that first torpid day, before taking off her kimono, she had lent me the book of Hypatia. Hypatia was a woman who lived in Alexandria fifteen centuries ago. She was amongst other things, a librarian, being custodian of the great library there. Books, you see, go back a long way. It was hand bound and battered, its hard cover embossed with age softened hieroglyphics – some goldleaf remained.

"I think you'll like this," she said, "It's very old and you are ... so modern."

I was sure then that she hadn't meant that as a compliment. In fact I took it that she had determined to educate me on the finer points of life, as if, being an illustrator, I was deficient in some respect. I had initially associated her too much with Sam, but surely a woman like Sorcha could not take that sugar daddy stuff seriously.

The Benefits of Tobacco

I had overheard the promises too, and thought as much of them as I now thought of the ones he had given me.

She told me not to scan the book, because, being an illustrator, that was the very first thing that I did. Back cover to front, always going the wrong way.

"Must I start at the beginning and end at the end?"

"It is a story." she snapped, "It never ends."

I wondered whether it was a true story – they are all the rage, you see; people these days are so suspicious about imagination.

"It will only become true if you read it. As far as you know everything else is a tissue of lies."

So, what happened in the end? Go on, then, skip through to that last page and read the lurid details there. I can see you furtively scuttling about those few bookshops that remain, thumbing through the murky past, dimly remembering some salacious reputation or a whisper you once heard in an adjoining cubicle. The dirty bits, the dirty bits are on page...

It all went wrong in the end, of course, for Hypatea I mean. It always goes wrong in the end. People just die, don't they? And Hypatia died painfully and spectacularly, flayed alive by the followers of a bishop. But worse again, perhaps, is the fact that she was forgotten, now that is a fate worse than death. Forgotten and scattered, and the great library of Alexandria laid waste, some people really have it in for books.

Sorcha was not of that mind that held that the Irish were riddled with guilt and anxiety concerning sex. Her research had not led her to that conclusion. Nor priest-ridden, although she had been.

"A bishop, in fact. They move diagonally, you know."

How those boyos, the bishops, have fallen. Time was they would have flayed Sorcha's flesh from her bones for thinking such thoughts, or is it that those times haven't changed all that much? All this was noted in her great book, a book inside her head like so many great books, from which she was given to lengthy quotation. One point which she made repeatedly was that we had not, as a race, matured.

Whether Sorcha matured over the time I knew her is hard to say. I knew she had ambitions for stardom, at least to become three dimensional and walk and talk on the silver screen, but by the last day she was still a model, a two dimensional thing. On that last day she was required to inspire me to produce a series of illustrations for the monthly feature, some awful pseudo-intellectual cant on sex and the machine. I had churned out such stuff so many times before but that was the trouble, my golden arm was growing rusty through overuse.

There are deadlines to be met on a magazine and Sam should be here to supervise them. But, lately his wife has exercised a peculiar hold over him, marriage, I think it's called. I was beginning to wonder how mine was going, there had been so many arched eyebrows of late, and late nights and cold mornings. I was picking up the phone to check, on this and other things, and to reassure Alison that really I worked in the most normal of environments about which I had no need to feel guilt, and not to wait up for me; but the phone was dead.

"What a night for death." I say.

"We're all dead outside of the stories we tell ourselves. In here – we live." Sorcha points to her breast. "Perhaps you live here." She raises her finger and pokes my head. "And the girl is willing and the girl is prone, and your hand

81

glides up the sheerness of her stocking..." She drops her hand and traces her nail along the ray seam of my jeans.

I panic. "*Stairway to heaven*," I say.

"What?"

"It's an old joke." I explain, "When a girl had a ladder in her tights we would call it the stairway to heaven."

"I know the song," Sorcha says, singing that part to where all that glitters is gold. "And it's stockings, not tights; God, you're so modern. Anyway, all the elements are in place, the chrome, the leather, the big blue emptiness of it all, the girl who is willing, the screen god flickering silver, the feel of silk. And everybody is waiting. And there is a part of you, no, not that part, a part of you wants to remember this in all its sticky detail. Why? For posterity, another sackload to fill your store of fantasy. But really you just want to tell the boys. Because this is the rite of passage and you pass by kiss and tell."

"So do you." I say. It's true, bit by bit, blow by blow, Sorcha has been filling me in with details of her past. I have yet to extract information concerning Sam, nothing useful; and the nearer I get the less inclined I am to pry. Is this what jealousy feels like, at birth?

Sorcha stands and twirls, too coquettish to be taken seriously, a little girl being her big sister, or is it the other way round..

"That's what I say to all the boys. I can only tell it to the boys because there are no men."

"Are we not men?"

"You're all stuck in the drive-in movie with your zip down and your best girl swimming in the long dead eyes of Jimmy Dean. That's where this town is, this whole country. Brigadoon where it rains every day. Stuck in the drive in movie with all its tyres flat, long after the credits have rolled."

"So, what keeps you here?"

"For the fantasy. It's all that's left. I have heard it called an open asylum as if that was the main attraction, but the real asylum is overseas, in the real world where they go mad on truth and talking straight and being direct. Big deal. The best thing to live is a lie, because it exercises the mind and keeps the body alert. And besides...

She smiles and yawns to show she has left the great book aside.

"And besides, it is a little project of mine. And I can shine a little sunshine through the rain."

So, this brings us to the point where I ask, what will I tell the boys? Should I tell them anything at all? The truth, the whole truth and nothing but the truth. But, so help me, I need to tell some stories first.

They are shooting a film on the seafront and the director, a friend of Sam's, wants to paint on a very big canvas. Whatever it is that the film was supposed to be about has been lost somewhere in the budget, somewhere between the scriptwriter's fees and the location director's daily expenses. So now the film calls for snow and although it is high, high summer, a summer unlike any we have ever seen here at Brigadoon; snow they will get.

Somebody with the technical know-how for these things arranges for a few tons of snow to fall on the town. It's all fake, of course. But the town looks so beautiful in snow and sunshine that you would wish it to always be like this. And it all melts so, so slowly and beautifully; only a flood could wash it all away.

That week the circus came to town. The circus came to town this time every year but this was a first in snowtime.

The Benefits of Tobacco

And this time it was bigger. The elephants were bigger; there was an elephant. The lions were bigger; there was a lion – but more of that later. What caught the imagination; and my imagination had sadly shrunk beneath succumbing to the spell of circuses, was that here for once east was not simply east nor west west, the twain did meet before our eyes. Africa on Arctic by the sea, oh, I just love this town.

When Sorcha had first entered the studio she presented me with her calling card. I was impressed and felt somehow complimented by the seriousness of her approach. Not that the card was po-faced by any means, it was colourful, modern, with a jolly Pierrot, a female pierrot, as the logo; it just made her and by extension me, seem so 'professional'.

After all, as I understood it, she was only there because Sam had found himself with his hand up her skirt at that awful performance fiasco; you do meet the most interesting people at these things, or so I'm told. Anyway, Sam had probably reasoned that he might get better acquainted by employing her to get her kit off in front of his house illustrator, perhaps he believed this guff about artists never becoming erotically inspired by their sitters. Perhaps he wanted to bypass all that awkward foreplay stuff and move straight on to the zipless fuck by way of promising her a part in his new movie.

"You mean business." I said.

She avoided the question and my groping eyes and asked instead if we had a screen. A screen?

"A changing screen. One that I can change behind." We did not have a screen because we did not have a model and had we ever had a model she could have changed in the john or the darkroom or there in front of whatever eyes she was going to spend the next few hours naked before. Perhaps she was really new to all this, but then, so was I.

She insisted. "I must have a screen. I am an artist's model, not a striptease artist."

"Can you change in the toilet?"

"Je-sus!" Then she laughed. "What sort of operation is this? If I stroll naked into a room I am a slut. If I strip before you, also a slut. An artiste. I am supposed to be a model. I must have a screen."

Ah, supposed to be. It wasn't that Sorcha was not or had never been a slut or a stripper but they were things she was only when she wanted to be, when she was supposed to be. She was an actress in the fullest sense of the word and her role was to be that of the model. The screen was in a way like the movie screen; in computer terminology it was the interface, and it was the wrapping. This was my gift wrapping for Sorcha, where, almost before my eyes she would change into whatever alter ego would be my muse for the day.

Occasionally Sam would take her out to lunch. Occasionally I would have to field questions on the telephone from Sam's wife. Occasionally Sam looked like he had slept on the couch, or in a ditch, but that was par for the course. What was peculiar was the fact that Alison had once or twice asked me questions concerning Sorcha, with eager fascination. How evasive was I then? Enough; each night I looked across the placid quilt at Alison's cold shoulder.

They are shooting a film on the seafront. It is a whimsical yet fantastic scenario of the arrival of a circus in a small town, as seen through the eyes of a twelve year old boy. That was Sam's idea, Sam is full of ideas, and what with the cast and crew and the circus people all drinking together on the seafront and Sam helping his good buddy, the director with the unpronounceable name, trace his Irish ancestry, it seemed like a good idea at the time for everybody to pool their resources.

The set is full of Americans, or people who would like to be taken for Americans; padded windcheaters, baseball caps, walkie-talkies – that sort of thing. At some stage you notice that they are talking more frantically than usual through their walkie-talkies, when the scene that they are shooting suffers a minor hitch. Camels grumble and acrobats tumble, chimpanzees chatter and the sawdust stinks, from a tent you hear the elephant bellow; but the lion, ah the lion, whom they had decided to film dramatically skirting the waves at gallop, has escaped.

So, Sorcha is here, and I am here, alone; and the building is isolated behind curtains of rain that join town, river and sea in a conspiracy of deception. And, as Sorcha paces and Sam fails to show, the germ of an idea grows inside my head and spreads throughout my body.

On the floor by my toe the discarded evening paper leads with the lurid HUNT FOR SEX FIEND, and a graphic of a man with rectangles for a face. But beneath my foot the second leader goes unnoticed; LION AT LARGE IN SEASIDE TOWN. Careless of me to take so little notice of that.

Sorcha takes a light from the butt of my cigarette, then drops the fag end with a hiss into a plastic cup half full with coffee.

"Thanks." I said, feigning annoyance, really I was finished with it just as I was finished with the half eaten corned beef sandwiches strewn on the table beside it.

All these half finished things, or half begun. It is, I suppose, like the optimist's cup and the pessimist's cup, half empty or half full. Me, I'm a diplomat, I just find myself in between, stuck in the middle.

Sorcha half smiles then kicks a filing cabinet and roars; "I'm bored!"

Tsk, I say, and flick through my book of nudes. I know Sam is late and, I suspect, drunk in some den with his director friend. He won't be coming but will instead leave me to look after the deadlines. Dead lions. Dead loins, perhaps, because something has crimped his ardour for Sorcha, or maybe it was only a casting couch. I doubt if there was ever any love to lose there anyway and, as Sorcha must be realising, little advantage to be gained.

"Rain, bloody rain. What kind of town is this? Yesterday it was covered in snow for this fucking film, fake snow up to your fanny and the sun splitting the rocks the day before. What sort of town is this."

It is a strange town, strange people. Outside, even in this appalling deluge, a motorbike roars into life – I think. Inside, I grow weary of airbrushing erogenous zones. I am wasting my time with acres of tangled limbs. When it all comes down everything is to be found in the face, all the beauty and the passion and the agony. That unique selling point, as Sam might say; the face.

I look at Sorcha and she looks at me. We are shallow people, we have about as much depth as the glazes of atomised paint from my airbrush. Everything is surface and what you see is what you get.

We stood at the open door for a while in the mist of the rain. The laneway was flooding and water lapped over the

The Benefits of Tobacco

kerb. Inside we embraced and waltzed, in a drunken sort of way, to the darkroom. The red light on, papers fluttered in the breeze; we fell into a dark ticker tape parade.

There was an old trick from college with which we amused ourselves. You needed to lie on the floor with your head centred on the baseboard of the repro camera and, eyes shut tight, take a quick exposure with the lens fully open. After processing, what you got was a dramatically graphic self portrait.

With Sorcha naked and the torrid heat, the incessant rain and the pressing deadline, it came to me, as these things do, to mix business and pleasure and spice up the old trick with sex on the floor, the snap to happen on the point of orgasm. I pressed the switch for the Repro and it came on with a low purr; something it shouldn't do but you will understand.

I explained myself and we did it – no thought of guilt or Alison or reconciliation. Sorcha went first with me on top, one finger on the button the rest all over her. Yes, she said, now, and in the searing light all was revealed; briefly in that moment I could make out the scars that held her face together. I had not come but it could wait, I processed the print and it was perfect; oh, the camera, the camera and the lies it tells.

Sorcha, lying there, laughed in a bittersweet way, "Now," she said, "it's your turn."

We shared a cigarette, as is traditional in these circumstances, and changed places. Now I looked up into the lens and waited. Sorcha, outlined by the safety lamp seemed to snarl as she sat astride me.

"Hush." she said.

I closed my eyes.

"Oh." she said, "Your nails. Yes, again, along my back, yes..."

There was something wrong here – my arms rested on the floor, one hand encircling an ankle. I eased my head a little off the baseboard and peered into the gloom, nothing, not even those dim shapes that usually become apparent in the dark. Something shaggy pressed against my foot. My jumper? Why then does it breathe? Something wet dripped onto my arm. Rainwater? But why so hot? I pulled Sorcha down to my chest, something she mistook for intimacy but really done to afford a wider view, and a pair of tawny eyes stared back at me from barely a yard's distance.

Sorcha moaned in what otherwise was a deathly silence and from beneath those tawny eyes, red shot in the safety lamp, came a low growl and I saw saliva shine on pointed fangs. The feral smell I had taken for sex was now simply feral.

I lay back. Sorcha was spent or at plateau and only barely moved to the most sublime of rhythms. Such was the pounding of my heart that at any moment I expected it to burst through its cage and shoot across the room. No thought of guilt or Alison or reconciliation; none at all.

So, there I was lying naked on a dirty floor, underneath a repro camera, beneath a beautiful girl, a hurricane blowing outside and an escaped lion sitting at my feet, one paw resting on my lover's back. You would think such a scenario would be so distracting as to make sex unlikely – but with my blood chilled solid by the fright I was frozen priapically stiff.

"Lion." I whispered.

"Yes," she said, with deep understanding, "Oh, yes."

The Benefits of Tobacco

No, lion, I tried, but the words wouldn't sound.

"Where?" Sorcha said, "Have you come?"

"Ooh." I said, totally distracted as Sorcha's pelvis moved to new and exciting rhythms. The lion growled.

"You are an animal." she said and bit my ear.

Against my buttocks: a pool of moisture and whether sweat, blood, saliva, cum, piss or the rising flood I cannot say and it doesn't matter, for truly it is irrelevant. The lion licked my hand and paradoxically it is this gesture which made my ardour decline. Unfortunately, Sorcha mistook the ebbing tide for orgasm and, as agreed, pressed the exposure switch to capture my ecstasy.

I would love to have developed that print, but I simply never got the opportunity. What did get printed, in a way, was my perspective of the darkroom. In that split second before I plunged into temporary blindness, the savage lamps etched the view indelibly on my retinas; it still looms at me every time I shut my eyes. As expected there was Sorcha in all her naked beauty, and the photogenic lion looking perhaps hungrier than I had hoped. But, what really chilled the marrow in my bones stood behind, framed in the doorway. A human voice raised, muffled with the storm and a figure of biblical proportions and haircut radiated vengeance and malice.

It was Sam.

It was a time that begged quiet, cunning and stealth. We got instead a "Holy Jesus Christ!" and the rest is all skin and hair and shrieks and roars. I'm not sure who Sam most wanted to kill but I guess that the lion was fairly indiscriminate. A flailing paw glanced my back as I rushed blindly towards where I remembered the door to be and I was sent sprawling into the reception area, the carpet squelching as I landed.

Sorcha told me later that the power picked that time to blow and so she saw little of the action. To make matters worse the dam beneath the volcano had burst and the lake had squeezed out through the gorge to join the rain-swollen river in the valley below. That too had burst its banks and swept murkily into the streets of the town. The first wave of muddy water sweeping through the door brought me round.

I stood petrified in the dark with the river up to my knees, the sound of fraught breathing somewhere off to my right and the lion chewing something in the corner.

I heard the lion leave after finishing his meal, which I briefly but fervently hoped had been Sam, and with his going my vision returned. I found Sorcha crouched like a wild Madonna in the recess in the studio wall and, after a terse embrace, decided to dredge the remains of our dear departed from the rising flood.

In fact Sam had escaped relatively unscathed, but concussed. A blow must have thrown him astride the camera where he lay prone, one leg dangling into the water. The lion had chosen my corned beef sandwiches instead.

We stripped him of his jacket and trousers which I put on. Sorcha had already put my leather jacket over her tattered robe; the rest of our clothes were destroyed. We carried Sam moaning to the back of the studio where we laid him in the coffin. I folded his arms as a mark of respect before wading back to the recess with Sorcha to await the dawn.

There, the sequence is right; the lion, the camera, the coffin, the flood. I let Sorcha's photograph fall to the floor, the last I'll see of her. I look over my shoulder to check for Sam, I am still haunted by that look I see when I close my eyes. But he is never there and I have not seen him since that night. I was half in a dream when I saw the coffin float past, Sam's face beatific and his arms folded, as the tide bore him majestically onto the street. I remember thinking, or hoping, that he might be carried out to sea; that somehow it would be nice for him to be tossed and turned forever on the ocean.

But that never came to pass. He did not sail away or die or anything romantic like that. His rage, I heard later, was to do with the fact that he had that night, out of love, arranged that role for Sorcha, fulfilling his end of the deal, whereas for her part ... Well, by some process of telepathy we agreed to shun all contact after that – we drifted apart, as partners often do.

Alison and Tara, my little cub, are still there, of course. I circle them as they orbit me. "Any port in a storm" Alison had said, in her enigmatic way. Later we made love on our bed and I thought it was the finest, the most exotic place. I lay awake for a long time afterwards listening as the neighbourhood cats yowled and the dogs barked, smoked a cigarette and watched the moon curve across the sky.

I told Alison the truth.

"Honesty," she intoned, "is the best policy."

I told her that it really was a lion, that a lion had mauled me in the dark.

She did not believe me either, not really. But at least she can learn to live with it; the truth will always out, is how the saying goes, in the end.

New Year's Eve

SNOW is hanging in the ochre air, hanging like Christmas on the purple birchtree branches. Silver birches against the silver snow, you see only their scars, the deep black stains that girdle their cracking barks. There is an awful pregnant silence that moans and scratches in the undergrowth, settling upon the season's garbage. That silence just won't go away.

There were happier days than this. There were days when our frosted breath commingled, puffs of white lace that hung and lasted like a kiss on the crystalline air. And our cracked lips just brushed, or smiled together at some implied joke, as our thoughts stroked each other unbidden, hidden behind the comfortable, sparkling silence. And you would turn away, temptingly, as we paused by some part-frozen water as if to take in the view, just so I could trace your quarter profile, new crescent of your cheekbones in the pale sun, slope of your neck from lobe to nape, just so you could turn and catch me and smile again. Better days than these, surely.

I should call you by your name. You are your name. It is the frame that holds the picture. At the very least it is that. It will be carved on your tombstone, and someday I may trace those deep, significant letters with my finger.

Evelyn lies here, it will say, or, simply, Evelyn lies. Sorry, I can't resist a joke. The Eve part suits you, since we found each other in a garden and became prey to temptation. But if you were Eve, I think you would have charmed the snake.

The Benefits of Tobacco

There is not much I can say about the end. I was there in the shadows, hidden, but I wasn't really there at the death. The death? It was Christmas time again and for a change there was a hint of snow and carol singers looked suitably red cheeked and cheery, though perishing with the cold. The last James saw of you was when you climbed that cavernous oak panelled, ghost laden stairwell at Balroddery to take a midnight bath. You had already taken too much to drink, so there was little new there.

James was alerted by the drip drip of water, cascading from the open bath through sodden carpets, floorboard cracks, joists and crumbling plaster into the scullery below, where he was having his nightly cocoa. He took the steps two at a time, heart pounding as his feet squelched on the carpet outside the door. Entering, he found...

Nothing, really. You had left the bath running, then left the bathroom. Still naked, or that's how I see you, you had descended that cavernous stairwell in the dark, walked through the drawing room and opened the French doors to float out into the night.

In the morning James found the body in the Secret Pond, that crisp circular pond gloomily hidden at the centre of the maze. They had to crack the ice to get through to it.

I was there for the funeral. I was not consumed with either misery or grief, you know how these things are. They are numbing affairs when you are not involved, guiltily scanning the hunched shoulders of the bereaved for signs of cracks, for cascading grief. In the crush of damp overcoats the rising frosted breath, chapped hands cupped over surreptitious cigarettes, people mutter, murmur, tell soft jokes as though they never cared.

James looked distant, hunted. I would have talked to

him had I been able, told him I was sorry for his trouble, which is not particularly original, I agree. But, in the gale swept panic of such contacts, they are the things that people say. Accepting words, consoling words, words no one can remember. Mind you, James and me are not on speaking terms, haven't been for a year. I can understand that. Had things been different, he might have justifiably attempted to strangle me, his eyes wild with murderous intent, or perhaps I am allowing too much rein to my imagination.

I greatly admired James's work. Everyone did. James was Prometheus on the river bank, lovingly moulding clay into exquisite human form, breathing life into the shapes he wrought. He could perform the same trick with graphite and paint, he could coax the spirit from cold stone, smooth it into jagged wood. Do I praise him overmuch? Perhaps. His head would swell still more if he was to read this, and that would be insufferable, but credit him this much at least, he was God to his own creation, a genius at the swirling centre of his own reckless universe.

You must have loved James, I suppose. After all, after all the grief, you returned to him, for a short while. It is true by that time he had done well for himself. No longer the dissolute artist, he was now the lord of the manor, in a manner of speaking. Yes, I know, James was still no more than a groundsman at Balroddery, looking out for the house and famous gardens of old man Devereux, expiring in his lofty turret. James clearly knew what he was doing, inveigling himself into the old man's confidence so that he rose from mews tenant to resident of the mansion's west wing. But your leaving had galvanised him, not just in provoking a feverish intensity in his own art, but also in the more measured, often flattering commissions which he undertook. Salon portraits, sweeping vistas of secret demesnes, classical pastiches. You always thought that type of work was fraudulent, and I agreed in so much as it helped belittle James in your eyes. But how much more genuine are the drips and daubs, the strings and wire, the detritus strewn floors that Malachy Mulkearns and his ilk parade smugly around the best galleries? No, let's be honest, James has talent.

Interesting that Malachy was the one to bring you back to James, though not before he had some hair of the bitch that bit. Pardon my French. It's just, it's just that ... well, I suppose that's how friendships go. I always thought that James and Malachy were all thick on the surface, all for show. You know how they disparaged each others work. That time you showed me Malachy's painting which had been a wedding present, hung in a surreptitious corner.

"A pearl of great price," you had said, with that way of sparkling praise, and a bitter twist of irony.

I mumbled that I loved the colours.

"You can buy colours in a tin!" James spat from the shadows.

Out here in the famous garden, with the moon a sharp sickle against the flat impassive sky, out here I draw a frosted breath and marvel at the view. The placid, long pond, the deep black flames of the solid stand of cypress trees, the ominous welcoming portals of the ancient maze. The science of such planning, its ordered exuberance and calm, the silent creep towards fruition and then the everlasting ageing; it is almost an insolence in the face of God.

I know my way through the maze. It is not too difficult,

as you well know, Evelyn. At the centre there is a circular pond with an ornate fountain surmounted by a hurrying figure of Mercury. A circular walkway is hemmed in by the high beech hedges with arched portals cut into it at regular intervals. There are twelve portals in all of which four are true openings that lead back to the maze. The other eight are blind recesses, four holding two seater wrought iron benches and four with Victorian cast iron statues. The statues were of pretty, idealised women, each one symbolising the seasons.

You are still out there somewhere, I can feel it. I see your footfalls on the frozen blue grass and follow. I see you drift past, a diaphanous veil against the gloom, I see you freeze. Then I remember. You had always told me that James wanted to immortalise you, but baulked at the task.

"Perhaps I am too beautiful," you said, without the faintest whiff of irony.

I should point out here that I am possessed of a strange and unique power. Put bluntly, I can freeze things in their tracks. I can stop the world, dead, and walk through it unobserved. How long can I keep this up? It is hard to say. How can I ever tell? How long is a piece of string? How long is a Chinaman. But I am pushing the envelope. I am taking it further and further and who knows how far I can go?

Anyway, I knew I would find you there. I always do. You have not yet begun to rust, although the passing seasons have left their stains. I have to laugh.

James had not lost sight of you after all, nor was his skill in any way diminished in its attempt to capture your beauty. In every detail you are exquisite, and I feel a quiver of jealousy when I think of the fun he must have had in making your mould.

I touch your skin. Cold metal. Gaze into your sightless eyes, brush against your swollen lips frozen in that supercilious smile.

"What are you doing here?", you demand, poised on your plinth.

I think back to when you first said that. One of Old Man Devereux's little soirees. Who were they to impress, really? Was Devereux showing his connections off to you and James, or was it perhaps, that he desired to show you off to the County? How could I know. I looked from pig to man and man to pig... but I am being unkind. It was a masked ball, appropriately set at Hallowe'en, when the air itself is on edge and the spirits are abroad.

"What are you doing here?" Briefly you let your mask drop so that I would receive the full force of your expression, ruby lips and flashing teeth, your pupils dilated to catch the starlight. I knew who you were, anyway. In your conceit you had fashioned your mask on your own face, a deathmask really, it was the one which James used for your sculpture I imagine.

"You should ask who I am and what I will do to you," I said, with a vague attempt at grandness.

You giggled and repositioned your mask. "Tell me who you are, then, gentle stranger." I could see through your Little Bo Peep demeanour and at last I knew, as I had suspected for months with every gauche reference, every lingering look exchanged on my visits to Balroddery. Just my luck to find myself, at the point of consummation of this long seduction, dressed in sixteenth century doublet and hose on a freezing November night.

Farce is the best antidote to feeling ridiculous, "I'm 'enry the eif', Oi am, Oi am." I sang. And you would be the first woman in four hundred years to fall for that line, you even seemed to lose your head, for a while.

Your clothes dropped off with surprising ease, and I wondered then how you seemed so impervious to cold. My own theatrical trappings didn't disengage quite so easily, and I had to rely on improvised apertures to make any impression on the love scene. This was a matter of some hilarity, and our lovemaking was not so perfect as I would have liked. Nevertheless, I can gild the memory a little.

You shivered.

"You'll catch your death," I said.

"I feel already, that in you I've caught a ghost," you said.

A couple of brief, hurried trysts followed in the maze, sustaining us over those Winter months. By Spring you had begun to walk into doors while I stopped receiving invitations to Balroddery. We became furtive, increasingly frantic – I was not, at that time, able to freeze time in its tracks. Easter brought a hiatus in the ongoing panic, a short idyllic sham when you moved into my basement flat on the grimy northern approaches of the town.

I suppose you were never made for downstairs life. Your disdain was subdued at first, then palpable. We lived like hermits, bread and bacon and cheap wine. Drunken hermits, the worst kind. The plans we made to attempt to arrest that downward spiral, a house in the country, in another country even, some form of escape.

Then there was Malachy's exhibition, a prestigious show in Dublin. That show was to be the makings of him, in more ways than one. So interesting, people said of the slashed and daubed canvasses. So wild, they enthused of the swathes of meaningless colours, so barbaric, they thrilled at the random spots and splashes.

"I like the use of colour," I said to him, with all the earnestness I could muster.

"I get it from a tin," he retorted, then turned to receive your fervent air kisses. Far too many kisses, I thought, far too little air between you both.

I attempted a joke. "Fact is, Malachy, you're so damned good with the brush I was wondering if you'd help us paint the flat." Malachy smiled with all his predatory teeth.

"Oh, really," you said, giving me that piercing look.

After that, Malachy, though now the toast of the art scene, became a surprisingly frequent visitor to the basement flat, sniffing at the dust, showing off his teeth. By midsummer he had stopped visiting and you were gone. It was amicably done, I'll grant you that, no stealing away in the middle of the night, no recriminations, no remorse. You would return to James, you said, who was lost without you, who was also it seems, set to benefit from the will of the near dead Devereux.

I suspected a ruse. By Autumn I was a furtive visitor to the famous gardens by night, catching glimpses of your rediscovered bliss in the lit windows of Balroddery. I was there that night and saw, saw the French doors open and the unlit Beamer cruise away up the gravel drive.

You never died at all of course. How could you? You were born indestructible, eternal, a permanent stroke of beauty against the grim background of existence. To me you were always an immortal, and deep down I knew I was never going to last. I knew we were never going to last.

I would like to say that I was making the grand gesture

when I died, but unfortunately my death had as much comedy as tragedy. I had come to take you home, in a way, in the sense that I fancied I could take the statue so lovingly wrought by James; stylised, ironically, as Winter. Oh alright, I was drunk, rat arsed pissed, as you'd say in your coarser moments. I am hazy as to the exact details, but I did succeed in prizing you off your plinth before the weight bore me down.

I can feel that power now. Everything is beginning to freeze. After a brief, drunken waltz, you slip from my grasp and shatter against the stone surround of the pond. Slowly, I see your beauty break to reveal its hollow core. I am plunged into ice and time stands still.

I see you at my funeral on Malachy's arm, just late enough for everyone to notice your entrance, early enough to seem somewhat genuinely in grief. I like the way you have made your eyes to seem so slightly bruised, and the dark funereal lipstick that gives your mouth that swollen and wounded look. You look very well, I think, I'm glad to see you there.

As for Malachy, well, you've found your perfect foil with his brutish mien. For some reason he is wearing a bandoleer, Viva Zapata, perhaps he is expecting a gunfight with James. Indeed, there is a palpable tension in the air, as you might expect. You had, after all, taken off through the French doors to be with your lover. True, you had taken precious few possessions, with the exception of the new red Beamer, James's pride and joy, which you wilfully wrecked at the pier gates. You also managed to flood the drawing room, an act of vandalism which very nearly put Devereux in his grave.

But he can afford it, you'll say. And James can be

forgiving. You've left him once before, and returned. And he is patient. But if I were in Malachy's shoes, those pointed alligator shoes, I would be careful in the deep, dead of night.

Snow drifts down from the parchment sky. It's a ticker tape parade for the empty streets. Some cars hiss by and a couple haul themselves uphill through the whitening northerly. Rose faced, they laugh at a shared confidence, arms linked and bodies huddling together. I observe from a distance, unseen, perched like a crow on the pavement's edge. At the top of the hill they pause, silhouetted against the snowblown sky, fading to white as the sun sets on the dying year.

Ante Meridian

OUTSIDE the window, far, far below, Europe rippled to the horizon, a grey, crumpled eiderdown over the sleeping continent. Victor had grown familiar with the view by now and, his fascination waning, glanced at the seat beside him. Grace was sleeping. She could travel like that. Whereas he had to see every new vista, each border surely crossed and each alien land uncovered, she could snooze her way to hell and back, emerging unsinged at the other end.

He fished inside his jacket, and opened his packet of long, black menthol cigarettes. Choosing one and lighting he drew deep and exhaled with nameless gratitude. Smoking or non-smoking? He had won the toss and scored another small victory in his war.

There was no point in him grabbing any shut-eye now. He inhaled, exhaled, and Grace murmured something in her sleep. Halfway to Athens, halfway to meet the shimmering sun. With haversacks on their backs and bags under their eyes, they would take a bus or taxi to Piraeus and choose. Choose one shimmering island amongst hundreds cooling in the sea.

He looked at his watch. Four twenty, ante meridian.

Hope was tired of jokes about her name. Hope springs eternal. Where there's life, there's Hope. But she couldn't really quarrel with her name, although, as simply 'Hope' there was the tantalising omission of the suffix. Was it hope-full, or hope-less? Both could apply, she supposed, as each implied a sense of failure in the past and an ill-defined expectation for the future. No, she couldn't really quarrel with her name.

Of all things, she looked forward most to the summer break. She looked forward in Hope. She always kept her destination a secret from others. It had become the subject of much speculation throughout the office, within the entire advertising agency where she worked. Account executives were known to speculate over a few drinks. Graphics would issue joke pamphlets: Hope bound for Italian Riviera, see Venice and Hope, etcetera. The telephone girls would lapse into speculation in those idle times between enumerating sexual conquests. Oh, they would wonder, where will Hope go?

One terse postcard would be the office's reward. Weather's lovely, it would tell them. Having a wonderful time. Wish you were here. Lies, all lies, or halftruths even. Always the implication that she was writing from within the cocoon of some loving ensemble, whether family generations in smiling bliss, or the giddy camaraderie of women of a certain age, once more in bloom beneath a caressing sun. Or even on the arms of some strong and silent male, his azure eyes amused at her girlish consideration at sending even such slight missives to the dull vipers at the agency.

We saw Florence yesterday, her copperplate would boast, visited the Uffizi, Il Duomo, the Ponte Vecchio. On another occasion: Greetings from Seville, The festival is in full swing. We saw a bullfight yesterday, so barbaric!

Amidst the idle gossip stronger opinions would be voiced, money would change hands, in all probability. In her mind's eye Hope could see the canteen crew and hear their talk. Felicity might be impressed, while Grace would examine the postmark with some disdain. "Ah, Naples."

she would say. "Sounds romantic but it's spaghetti with no meat."

Another, Peter perhaps, would crack, "Maybe she wants a drop of the crater." D'ye get it? Crater? Vesuvius? Victor, she imagined, would keep his counsel. Venal Victor, visualiser of commercial fantasies who always stood so close when reviewing her progress on the drawing board. That scent was with her yet, a cocktail of aftershave, sweet cigarettes and suppressed sweat. Oh, thought Hope, at least she was getting away, and the petty politics and oh so polite probing could wait for another day.

Three hours out and three miles high, Hope was poised at the apex of her outward journey. Downhill all the way, she heard herself say and, devil that she now was, took a pack of filter tips from the prim shoulder bag poised upon her lap. She took one, lit, inhaled grey smoke and exhaled sultry blue.

Grace was having a bad dream. All dreams, thought Grace, are bad. It was not that she was a practical person to the point of soullessness. Oh no. Her talent in the field of art was legendary throughout the advertising agency. She could wield pen, pencil or paintbrush with such precision and flair, capture any reality with ease, within deadlines, well within budget. Agency clients, between beer commercials, shampoo campaigns and tantalising marketing strategies, were always keen to commission Grace's moonlighting talents. From stacks of photos she could create for hard pressed executives their perfect, hyperrealist family, all teeth and airbrushed embraces, clutched in bonds of permanent union about some totem of executive achievement – the mahogany desk in the booklined study, with Flicca the pony at the country villa, draped lovingly around the chrome charisma of the XJ7. Such a family, such possessions, such admirable dental care, that any managing director would be proud to have, even to meet every now and then. But in default, Grace's version would stare benignly down from the office eyrie, another trophy to prove their worth.

Grace was having a bad dream. She dreamed in black and white. This wasn't an inability to dream in colour, it was just that monochrome movies were so much more artistic, don't you think? She dreamed of the silken, black and billowing sea. She was skinny dipping for the benefit of some beach party hidden in the dunes. Now frozen and inflamed, she ran across the coarse, mica shimmering sand to the mingled sounds of angelic laughter and the guttural rutting of a half familiar beast.

She crested the dune to find her exhibition had been in vain. Couples had paired off, eloquently, two by two, into some ark that would carry their seed inland to the golden future, their hands and lips and flesh flowing together like mercury, quicksilver. And where was her lover? Her one and only love, for now at least. There, the beast on all fours and some tinkerbelle clinging beneath, clawing at the broad raw muscles of his back. Who was beneath? Her, perhaps? She leaned closer to look, and screamed.

Victor heard her murmur in her sleep. He bent closer to hear. Menthol smoke curled about her parted lips. Victor, he thought he heard her say, Victor. And Victor smiled his knowing smile.

It was a winning smile, in every meaning of the word. Victor would wear it into the conference room to clinch the most slippery of deals. He wore it to accept awards. He wore it when he first commissioned Grace to paint a picture of his perfect family. It was all he wore in the locked and empty, almost empty, boardroom, the murmur of the office party far, far below – it was all he wore bar his patent shoes and paisley socks as Grace explored other distant, hairy reaches of his body with her lips.

They had been discreet about the affair. Within the office there would be some surreptitious rubbings and fondlings, sweet nothings whispered. They would arrive separately at their secret rendezvous, closer but still cool over a couple of drinks, then, in the short moment of heat, steaming up her car afterwards. They had to get to Athens, get away from it all.

As Victor raised his head from his sleeping mistress he allowed his eyes to scan lazily across the cabin, along the aisle, perhaps to catch another pair of eyes admiring this handsome couple. Some five or six rows back his pupils dilated, and his smile faded.

We all live in Hope, in a way. Some bizarre, yet common sequence of atoms inherited from the primordial ooze, links us and all living things. But mostly us. So across a crowded concourse, in the confines of a coffee shop gazing idly at the street, it is the face you see and admire that glances up to catch your stare. Connections are made, contracts exchanged, vows of silence taken.

No words were exchanged, nor indeed did any outward sign of recognition pass between Hope and Victor. It was as if they didn't know one another, had never met, were different people entirely from those dull and distant doppelgangers at the agency. In a way they were.

Every country feels different, smells different, is different. It's not just the diesel, the jet lag and the duty free; the air itself is the breath of strangeness. Victor,

The Benefits of Tobacco

Grace and Hope each became aware of that subtle but accelerating change, the shedding of that everpresent weight which was the accumulation of life and work and dreams. It is not the past which is like a foreign country, the past is always the same. Familiarity is in the past.

A bus takes them across the tarmac to the terminal. Grace, soft eyed from sleep, has been appraised of the danger. She stands, holding the metal bar, only a few feet from where that darkhaired woman of a certain age, gazes fixedly into the airport dawn through her dark shades.

They have passed and not spoken. Eye contact has been brief and flitting. When Hope put on her sunglasses she blotted out that place called home. Victor is not so ashen faced now. Dishevelled, hair loose and streaked with the first fingers of dawn, for Grace he cuts a surprisingly rakish figure. He bends to murmur in her ear.

"Do you think that Hope is blind?" he asks.

Grace smiles. "She'd want to be blind." she says.

He shrugs. "I'd rather she was dumb." he says.

Grace slips her hand inside his jacket, caressing him. Deaf, dumb and blind, she thought, more like love, really. She reaches up to kiss him and is surprised that he doesn't resist. They kiss.

In baggage reclaim there are enough people, and space, to ensure that distance is maintained. The deceit is made real. Still, the couple watch Hope as she leaves, alone, through the arrivals door.

"Do you think she's alone?" Grace asks.

But Victor isn't sure, which is unlike him. "You mean lonely?" he checks.

"I just wondered, that's all." says Grace.

Victor brightens, jokes that perhaps Hope has a lover

here. A Greek shipping magnate, perhaps, or a waiter. Grace makes a racist remark, then they lapse into silence. Perhaps Hope did have a hidden lover. A passionate affair, or sordid, who knows? As they leave the building Grace laughs. Victor looks at her, concerned. She anticipates the question and reassures him. "It's nothing," she says, "Just a secret."

Hope dreams on behind her shades, oblivious to the breakneck speed the taxi takes towards Athens. It could be any city with its bustle and its noise, but she would seek and find the silence there. There. Her lover would emerge from a recess in the colonnaded square. Smiles on their lips, then their lips on their lips. Brushing, knowing, anticipating. The clock on the cathedral tower would swing through that last hanging minute, wiping the square clean of tourists and hawkers, and their gawking, intrusive vulgarity. The clock would chime into the hanging silence. Midnight, midday, what did it matter, really? Ante meridian. Post meridian. In the space between the seconds, between time itself, she would take her lover's hand and see her smile, and they would link each other loosely and walk their swaying walk, across the ancient cobbles into the secret city.

A Day

OR a newspaper page, unfolded, floated on the air
devils, borne upwards into the lamplights and
the brown glowing sky. Yesterday's paper,
yesterday's story circles upwards and outwards, turning
and turning like a ragged magpie that steals into the night.
In a darkened doorway a cigarette tip burns and twists,
above the kebab house a neon fizzes and dies.

There are shouts in the night, people called Eric, and
Two Bar, and Keogh make their names famous to a few
ears. Samantha giggles as fingers search for the warmer
skin beneath her cellophane wrap. Samantha is wrapped
up tight and won't yield.

"Go on."

"No."

"Go on."

"Noooh."

The fall against the shutters sends their thunder through
the red brick canyons. Bandits on horseback blink away,
briefly, and grow bored again.

"Go on."

"No, not here. Not now."

Not yet, perhaps? Well, where then? Cooling asphalt and
discarded wrappers, rare taxis swishing to exotic places:
Tamango's, Fandango's, Flamingo's, or some such names.
Sky burning red, burnt at the edges, skinny wires
humming, slung between silver poles.

Luke probes through the words, sniffs the pungent scent
of surrender, raises predatory nostrils towards the westerly
weaved into the stale air pushed out from the bellows of
the city. He is aware of the cold creeping in, the first damp

thrill of morning. A joke occurs, the one about the beggar woman who fell asleep outside the synagogue and awoke...

Samantha pulls away and...

Awoke with...

"Just a kiss then." Oh, why did he say that? Or is it more than the cold and damp, more than the sickness of beer and far too many cigarettes?

With a heavy lidded stare, Samantha assents. With bad grace.

Luke sees an ash tip flare. Flare and fall. The third person.

"Not here, not now." Softer, Samantha considers. "If you had a place to go, a car even..."

It's 5am in Amsterdam and this is how I know...

Driving through the darkness on the outskirts of town, Michelle Shocked playing on the stereo.

It's 5am in Amsterdam and ...

Past the silo, the schoolhouse and the watertower.

"Is that record stuck?"

I pull a cigarette pack from the folded sun visor, and take one.

"Mid morning ambience, Matt, go with the flow."

It's 5am in Amsterdam...

"Jesus." Lighting up, looking through narrowed eyes at the old dancehall on the outskirts of town. "Bit of blow would be nice, though."

I narrate a slice of my life, a joke, as draper's shops and shuttered pubs loom out of the night. The streetlights ahead simmer, somewhere, an electric toothbrush hums. "Met this gayboy in the Green onetime."

"Oh, yeah?"

"Said he'd give me a lift out to Ranelagh and we'd drop

112

off at his place..."

"Whaa?"

It's 5am in Amsterdam...

"I didn't know he was a gayboy. You know me, straight down the line, Mr Ordinary Powder. But, there was a little misunderstanding..."

"Yeah, right."

"When I asked him did he fancy a blow..."

"Fucking faggots. Worse than the knackers – come and camp in smaller places."

There was an encampment on the outskirts of town which we had passed, surprisingly, without comment. Trailers and ghosts in the embers of a campfire, a snowbound TV sending out static.

It's 5am...

Past the draper's, the butcher's and the baker's; past the Memorial and the Post Office, a good scattering of shuttered pubs and Flannery's Fast Food. Flannery's Fast Food assuring us of the fame of Flannery's Flaming Taco, Flannery's Doner Kebab.

"Fastest food in the west." After silence, I enlarge the point. "They'd be the Flannery Brothers of Kilfenora; Paschal, PJ and Mustapha."

"Mustapha piss." I should explain about Matt. "Where's the fucking hostel?" Prone to exercising the expletive. "Dead as doornails," entertains cliche. "The whole town is dead," inclined towards extremes.

It's 5am in Amsterdam...

"Oh, shut up." Impatiently silences the stereo.

There are so many different lexicons, and all the time we are striving to make a connection, to arrive at that sequence of words and phrases, of namedrops and

113

nuance that mutually reveals another of our own tribe. We're out there in the tall grass, all the time, like the joke, jumping up and down shouting: 'Where the fuck are we?' Only now and then colliding with another who speaks the same language.

I remember the homosexual's record collection. Jungle Book and Grease, more scions of good cheer like James Last, Top of the Pops, Frank and Elvis's Vegas days. Badfinger. Badfinger was about as good as it got. There were records by people I didn't know, people whom nobody knows, people nobody would admit to knowing after releasing such ghastly records.

I remember thinking at the time how creepy it was to have records like that lying around your spiral carpet. Surely no one bought records like that, for themselves. Yet, there they were, and as I flicked through desperately searching for sanity a shadow fell over the room.

I remember furtively checking the ceiling for hidden cameras.

I am not the first person to take the long way home. I am not the only tourist of life to have lost my baggage at some infernal airport connection out in the desert. Out here. Deep in the arsehole of nowhere...

Before I could get to the point the car slewed around a corner into a half hearted main square. We skidded to a halt, briefly surprised to have gained the centre with so little trouble. Matt can get lost in the suburbs of the smallest village. Looking for water, he'd climb a hill.

"Let's ask directions."

As if in answer, a westerly blew up, sending a ball of tumbleweed across the square, where, after snagging on a bench, a post box, it rolled away down Main Street. I pointed out that we only had to wait two hours or so and maybe get an early breakfast. A coyote called.

"We could ask the hippy on the roof, though."

A hotel butted on to the square and all across its ground floor facade was a glass front extension. The black, implacable windows of the first floor gazed into the darkness. Poised between, though poised may be too strong a word – splayed across the flat roof of the extension, one leg dangling into space, was the hippy in question.

Perhaps hippy is too strong a label. He had long hair and a full beard, he was unremarkable in attire, however, and when he spoke there was nothing in his modulation to single him out as belonging to this, or that, tribe.

"Hey. Oi! Fucker on the roof..."

"That will win him over."

"Any place to stay 'round here? Anything open?"

His position remained prone, but his head swivelled around and he regarded us for a moment with a mixture of horror and bewilderment.

"Are you okay up there?"

Matt clicked his tongue in irritation. Perhaps he was hoping that the conversation would pass off as if everything was in order. As if, on any given Friday in any given one horse town at five o'clock in the morning or thereabouts, two strangers might be expected to strike up polite conversation on the features, attractions and accommodations of said one horse town with the nearest available drunk hanging off the first floor of the hotel.

The hippy had questions of his own. He had issues. Did we intend staying in this town? Why? Did we have a key for his hotel? Why not? Without changing position, which must have been uncomfortable, he shared some advice with us.

"You've got to get out of this town, man. They'll eat you alive in this town. I've only been here a day, man, and I can tell you something... They're all the same. All the fucking same. I tell you, it's not like you can see they're painted in woad, but you know they are. This is one weird fucking town, man..."

We assimilated this information in silence. We glanced about, nervously, expectantly; there was in his speech a note of the approach of imminent danger. It wasn't just that the natives were restless, they were like the blood-dimmed tide, an inexorable force, and we found ourselves in the hollow silence as that first wave drew back and prepared to launch a breaker onto the beach.

"I've just got to get into my room and grab a few things." He shook his head, overwhelmed by sadness. "Then I'm out of here, I'm telling you. Me and Phil there, we're fucking gone, man..."

"Phil?"

"Yeah, Phil, down below me here, on the street. You alright, Phil?"

The name of Phil echoed through the silent canyons. More tumbleweed blew in from the west. Whooooo-ooooohhhh.... I looked at Matt and Matt looked at me. The horror, the horror. If we kept driving we might see the dawn on the ocean. We could pull the cold fire of the east with us, pull it over us like an eiderdown, sleep until the cold and damp crept in, parked above a stormy cove.

"It's 5am in Amsterdam..."

"You see, it's catching."

You told me once that you were a different person. You

weren't always an explosion in a fireworks factory. You weren't always an incendiary device. You were shy, introverted, bookish.

"Saturday afternoons, summertime, anytime the sun was shining and time was... free. I'd take a book out onto the green, this green patch on our cul de sac. There was a beautiful old tree there. I think it was a lime tree. Big and regular, like a cartoon tree, with these deep green leaves, slender twigs. It was always like it was drooping down, that tree, melting in the sun. Anyway... I suppose the other girls, other boys, would have something physical going on. Don't laugh. It's not like they were frigging on the grass or anything, this is middle class Dublin in the mid seventies – for gawdsake. Physical, whistling, slouching, chasing a ball around, playing the ghetto blaster too loud. But me..."

Ah, me..

"I just loved to read. Dickens, Hardy, Hemingway, Yeats even. Moby Dick, I remember reading Moby Dick... You, honestly! Call me Ishmael. They called me Specs, or the Professor was another one... Yes, I did, but I don't wear them now, although I need to. Blind, I am, like love."

That laugh, that most welcome of all infections. The pleasure it was simply to sit within the sound of your voice, at all times. Happy, sad, sulking sometimes, as the passionate must. And all the time the imagination turning like an engine – what was it like to be another person? What was it like to be you?

You're walking again, through suburban streets striped with cartoon trees. You clutch a book to your breast and all its words are mingled there. You are aware of being watched but only give notice as you reach the corner. A slight turn, a swivel of the hips, the hint of a smile. You disappear.

The long talks we had in the car, these are things which corrupt my memory in curious ways, playing mean tricks. The smell of petrol on hot asphalt. A tinny radio playing a certain song. A sudden reflection in chrome. Cigarette smells and upholstery.

I would like the sadness of a sudden, stark tragedy. An explosion in the fireworks factory. We parted over dinner and drinks, as these things sometimes do. Returning from that weekend, that disastrous fling where everything we had was thrown to the savagery of the four winds. In the morning what appeared at first to be satisfaction turned to remorse and silence set in with the journey east.

At a truck stop cafe, which was bright, efficient and clean, I had an accident with the sauce bottle that covered most of my plate in ketchup. The waitress was apologetic and a new meal promised.

"Very nice," I said.

"They'd want to be. It's hardly your fault, after all."

No laughter, that was the hint. Fish and chips swimming in a red sea. Tepid coffee and cigarettes, the miles home in silence and regret.

For days I sat and looked at the telephone as though it was being deliberately obstinate. I juggled numbers in my head until I thought that I would go mad. Then it all began to ebb away. I saw you one time in a seaside town. You drifted along the crowded promenade in that oblivious way of yours, in a skimpy summer dress and more suntan than is natural at these latitudes. You always looked after yourself, for yourself, but also for the adoration it brought. You said to me once: "My body is a temple, yours is a kebab house."

A Day

The seabreeze caught your skirt and blew, but softly, and there was a gracefulness about the scene, about you, which I could admire objectively. I could feel good about it and in an instant I let my eyes flicker on, across the sea and stony strand and along the crowded grassy Esplanade. Drawn then upwards by a shrieking triangle of parents and child, the father flying a kite in the turbulent sky, swishing it expertly about like a bird of prey

5am in Amsterdam is from the album The Texas Campfire Tapes by Michele Shocked (Cooking Vinyl, 1986)

The Aeroplane Trap

GABRIEL had a flame for one of the German students. It was not like him. Despite his easy way with women he was essentially of the type that would naturally be referred to as a bachelor – interest but no infatuation, intent but without purpose. With Petra I could see the attraction. She came in most days, sometimes to read, sometimes to surf the net, but at all times a contained tempest of suntan and silvery detachment. She was, as were most of the best and brightest, taken under Gabriel's golden wing but his charm was slightly blunted in Petra's case by the persistent weakness of her English. Meanwhile his ardour was further stoked by her silence.

As the flame burnt ever brighter, Gabriel developed the notion that I was fluent, or at least conversant, in German. I came to represent to him the key to unlocking Petra's stony citadel.

I have no idea how I happened to impart such an impression. Perhaps Gabriel was impressed by my frequent flying hours in a lifetime of package and backpack holidays. He was a homebird, a necessary condition given his dislike for modern modes of transport, his fear of flying. Yet the fact remained that my linguistic powers were almost entirely confined to English – my Irish was poor, my French lousy, my German non-existent!

Perhaps not entirely non-existent.

As a residue of those backpacking days, in the forced camaraderie of Europe's hostels, filed away there amongst the blurred friendships, one night stands and delirium tremens, there is a sentence:

In meiner freizeit ich mache gern model flugzeuge.

I happily gave this to Gabriel as a bauble with which he might impress the fraulein. He easily committed it to memory and took some supplementary advice on delivery. Make eye contact and maintain it, I advised.

"In meiner freizeit ich mache gern model flugzeuge." Gabriel pauses. "I trust it's not something rude or gross."

"Not at all," I assured him.

"It wouldn't give offence?"

Even in these politically correct times, I could not see how it would give offence.

The next day I was in the History section for rather a long time. I was correlating the French Revolution and Romantic poetry. Bliss was it in that dawn to be alive, I read; perhaps with appropriate prescience as I spied Gabriel striding down the aisle towards me.

"You cunt," he said, amiably.

"But to be young was very heaven," I continued, aloud, then asked him how he had got on with Petra.

"She thinks I'm an anorak!"

"But you are an anorak."

Gabriel paused only briefly. "Model aeroplanes, for fuck sake!" It was unlike him to curse. "What can she think of me now?"

It was true, I suppose. Petra's attitude had subtly changed, loosened even. But the smirk that played on those subtle lips was not the smile of invitation. She was greatly amused, fondly amused, but alas nothing more.

"Model aeroplanes." Gabriel sighed.

"But only in your spare time. Don't you see? Don't you find it... enigmatic?"

"I don't recognise spare time, you bollix." (Okay, he knew some regular swear words.) Gabriel stuck out his chin, aggressively. "And what do you do in your spare time?"

And what do you do in your spare time?

In truth, much of that was taking up with smoking and drinking. There was also thinking, thinking being alternatively devoted to, these days, Aristotle's *Poetics* and their relevance to modern theatre and Isabella's body. I don't here disavow Isabella's mind, wondrous fascinating and deeply engaged on most of our meetings, but not thought about in absentia with the same desire as I thought about her body.

I lay with Isabella on a silver strand. She said she liked to paint the Great Bear on the chest of her lovers. White pinpricks against the dark skin. Ursa Minor too, Orion if the fancy took her.

"It is a hobby of mine and I can be both angel and slut." She has to explain. "As an angel I fly among the stars. As a slut I've been fucked by the northern hemisphere."

I was enchanted. Here was a symmetry between love and aesthetics which I had not suspected. Yet, for all that there was the question of the words used. The right words. "And what does the true lover say?" I asked.

"There are so many, Europe is a big country."

"Just one line then, one line from the perfect lover."

She bent over my shoulder. In the cusp of silence, between the thumping of the surf, she whispered in my ear. In my pink shell...

The Benefits of Tobacco

I DREAMED I was. No. I dreamed I was somebody else and I was to meet a girl from Leinster Road – the girl in the fur collared coat whom you see shivering in the cold as she waits for the bus into town; her breath beauty in itself, like the practised art of a smoker. Or you see her walking arm in arm with her friend, past the Baptist Church on Saturday mornings, on down tree lined streets towards Rathmines.

You know the girl I mean: mid twenties and mousy hair, the face of a porcelain angel. But it doesn't really matter if you do or not, the point is that it is only because I am somebody else that I have chanced to be intimate with her in some way. At least, so I must presume.

I was to meet her, for either the first or last time, maybe even some time in between, in a breath-fogged, goldfish-bowl cafe in Rathgar. The cafe takes its morning trade from fluorescent clad workmen – sausage and egg and cream buns, burnt tea and cigarettes; by lunchtime to be replaced by students in scarves and coats – salads and choux pastry, roll-ups and good mocha coffee. By late afternoon it's terminally quiet with tired shoppers and commuters but it remains, eternally, the nameless cafe. Still, I am clearer about the cafe than about myself, or herself, or ourselves, but I've not been able to find it since. Perhaps it turned into the same sort of sanitised clinic they've all become.

I have decided on our conversation in advance: that it must be witty with the faint whiff of innuendo, the sort of well poised tableau that would thrill any artist or budding tragedian, yet grace the cafe with laughter and whispered nothings. I spin a web that sees us spend winter afternoons in cinemas and basement bars, arguing the merits of film noir, the limits of love and the benefits of tobacco.

As I move within the ambit of her breath, am enveloped in the sense of her scent and feel the warmth radiate from her frost scorched skin I find myself poised, unexpectedly, on a tightrope where below the crowd gathers round to contemplate eternity. I am aware of the tiniest detail and the vast expanse of being. Some things elude me. Her name eludes me when we meet. I have difficulty with my own until she repeats it twice.

"Adam, oh, Adam."

I notice her nose, pinched pink from the winter, remember the poster Bieres de la Muse on the wall of her bedsit, recall the smell of patchouli and percolated coffee. I gaze past her shoulder to the cold ochre band of the horizon, behind a lacework of naked trees. I see birch bark whipped black and white and return to the warmth where carbon and tobacco breath spread, searching for heat in the evening rush hour.

Now, I remember, we were breaking up.

Something ghastly. Portents on the evening news. Those well known purple tones that speak in trusted epigrams amidst the static and swirling spokes of the evening rush hour. She glances at the sky, looks for touchstones in the architecture, some subtle sign of recognition in the spires, the slanting glass concourses, the cavorting gargoyles. Above it all billows the green, giant copper dome, golden cupolas, granite barbicans; beneath it all the hum of neon boiling chrome, footfalls for home past whispering, suggestive pubs.

She looks for her face, is surprised by her face in sudden mirrors, wonders if the occasional surreptitious looks she receives are from those who share her face or maybe from those who have possessed her.

Body and soul. She sees the stack of offices, flourescently lit, and lightly clad workers taking files to the photocopier. Sees them photograph her face a million times until toner hangs like cordite in the air after a fireworks display, then the shredder turns the images into ticker tape and showers it like confetti on the crowds below.

She is reflected in the raindrops, and in the standing pools they fill. She wonders if this process of replication, of exterior possession was visited on the other faces she saw in the crowd, but guesses not. Even if similarly fragmented: to each their own jigsaw, to each their own eggshell.

Street sellers swirled in the breeze at the station's entrance. Pavement artists sent fathomless perspectives plummeting to infinity beneath the city floor. Birds flew. On one wing of the Financial Services, a fuse blew.

She takes coffee just off the station platform. She notes that the headlines promise war but consoles herself that it will most likely be very far away. At the only other occupied table sits a vaguely familiar young man whom at first she presumes to be reading, then realises he is writing in a diary. He stops and lights a cigarette. She feels a pang, of hunger, perhaps. She curls her spoon in the cappuccino foam. Where the station shed meets the sky duck egg blue and shimmering steam, where the station shed ends she sees a painting in her memory and can't quite place it ...

Colette is buried in her book. She is a Russian doll

wrapped around and around a dozen plots, each featuring her as the main protagonist. Her lips part and kiss with the prose, her virginity is plucked and grows and flowers again; and again she is buried in the brown earth of the pages. Every so often her pale blue eyes rise from the printed page, with resentment, with hurt, and see a universe as intensely as she has always seen it, only each time it has been subtly changed from her previous stolen gaze.

She wonders, yes, sometimes she remembers even, how the world looked before she found herself in reality pressed between the yellowed pages holding a strangers words – an invisible flower, an unnoticed scent. Mostly she forgets. Where before, the universe was phrased in terms that did not recognise the shapes transcribed by the lovers on her page, nor know the indentations these lovers left on furniture, the shapes they made of fabric and shadows left behind on street corners and parks; now it implicitly acknowledges such chimeras as fact, a hidden part of the history of this projection show she reluctantly and sporad-ically views.

She knew that it was not a case that to observe is somehow to create, there was also that subcurrent of thought and text that combined to make the broth. Still, Colette did not know quite how she achieved this. She was still aware that she had no place in the outside world, beyond her pages and peripheral vision, she was essentially the stuff of smoke and mirrors. There was no recognition of her there, no reconciliation. Yet, the act of creation was a secret she knew, like the ancient gardens near the Bishop's house, accessed through that old rusty gate. There, by whispering in the lock 'I love you,' it would always open to her with a greasy sigh.

The Benefits of Tobacco

She is walking in the street in chime to the million footfalls of strangers. The dull drum of walking falls unexpectedly into step and a weird resonance rises above the regular redbrick to the painted powdery sky. There is a breath on her shoulder where she pauses, where she pauses to consider buying a cup of coffee from the hatch across from the Cathedral.

"Colette! Colette?"

She turns and lets her recognition flow, although no name comes to coincide with the face. Still, she knows.

> In old Dublin town,
> At the corner of Derby Square,
> See Frida Kahlo and Fred Astaire.
> Dance the lobster quadrille.

Of what did we talk? Of old times. Of the times when first we did something and this in itself was something of a first, though also the last time we would share such intimacies together. There was an incident she recalled, prompted by the inevitable query: your first kiss.

"I was very young," she said.

"Sweet sixteen?" I asked.

"Younger still, but still ribbons and curls. It was the boy next door, of course. There was some waste ground beside our house and that was the jungle to us, a place we'd go to explore..."

"Explore?"

She rolled her eyes and reminded me she had said younger still, and speculated that I sounded jealous. She continued:

"I can't remember if there had been any serious intent, or how serious his attentions were. But I remember one day that we stopped after our run through the jungle and

129

he was standing there and he was taking a piss but didn't quite turn away..."

"You could have averted your gaze," I pointed out.

"Well, I didn't. Anyway, he said 'look at this', maybe to do some trick with the fountain, I don't know, and ended up spraying some vaguely in my direction. I reached out and pushed him and he toppled, his thing still trickling, into a bank of nettles. Man, how he roared."

"I thought we were talking tenderness and first love," I said.

"Well, it was the tender flesh was stung, but I was really sorry about that, I mean, I felt awful. It just seemed ...out of proportion..."

"Swollen, I'll bet."

"Honestly," she sighed. "I was sorry and, you know the old saying, kiss it and make it better?"

"You didn't!?"

She laughed. "You should see your face. No. I said I would kiss him and make it better and that's what I did. It was nice, tender, the smallest hint of tongue. Mind you, he never put his firehose away and when we broke for air and I looked down..."

I told her I didn't want to know. I told her there were pictures of her that I would treasure but that this did not look like being one. She was surprised I was so squeamish.

"Life's just like that," she said. "It's an eruption, a tumour on perfection. You want to hear sweet music as the final credits roll, you want to check out the soundtrack album. You think you can come through these encounters unscathed, like fitness freaks think they can die in the picture of health. It never happens like that. As for Barry, ah, poor Barry. Our family left the area shortly afterwards, perhaps it was just as well and Barry, last I heard, took off for South Africa. See, there is a connection, I just knew there would be a pattern – jungles!"

"More savannah, I would think..." I trailed off, it was close enough.

She shrugged. "Anyway, I see him there all khaki and bronze, the Great White Hunter, Stuart Grainger or something, or maybe more Daktari in the end because he was there to save lives, animal or human I can't recall. Or that was the story."

"In the end?" I asked.

"I heard he died in an accident on safari, nothing spectacular, just an overturned jeep or some such. Poor Barry."

> *Somewhere out there,*
> *Off in the cold distance,*
> *Someone calls for help,*
> *Or at least for assistance...*

A couple in a rented room, so near the street as to reach out and touch the feet of passersby. A couple coil in coitus. Sallow and sepia shapes gyrate in the gloom, sweat sparkles and sprays from their skin and slowly, slowly they are caught in a diagonal beam of buttery light, and slowly the light fades and dies.

You have seen paintings like that, caught between the fire and ice; Caravaggio or Vermeer. Ageless things that continue their surreptitious life the instant you glance away.

Resting back on the sheets, he turns to look at her. He is glad he has selected her, for so he feels he must have

The Benefits of Tobacco

done, from when he first discerned the pearl's grain beneath the pure to this perfect moment, this most in-depth study of her sexual architecture.

She will only remember, only remember lying back on the sheets of a very large bed. She will feel him flow in and out and think of it as nothing or as the eternal sea.

His essence, in and out.

"Been there," she thinks, "been there, done that, worn nothing at all." She will take a cigarette from the jacket hung at the head of the bed. His or hers, it hardly matters. Lighting up, she will take her breath in again and then with the faintest echo of her orgasm push the smoke upwards to the ceiling. She will let the moment linger.

"I like it when time stands still," she will look at him from under her lids. "Lover?...", and all around is darkness and silence. "It's funny when you think of it, all the things we do that others say are so bad for us. With people even. 'He's so bad for her,' they would say. So bad for her. How can they know, hmm? How can they? Lover?"

You hear the rush of her breath again in the darkness, smell the burnt air and all the things that have passed. Her voice continues inside your head. "These things are so bad for us, so bad; but the benefits we get from cigarettes..."

At last I remember, clearly and distinctly, in that last sip of coffee before the train pulls in to the platform. The electronic clock flashes and time stands still.

It was out of crowds, and smoke and chrome she came. Then I first saw her take that highheeled tightrope walk to the table where I sat alone. Partly breathless, tragically poised, she asked intensely for a light. I cupped my fingers to the flame to shield it from an imagined wind. So, it was thus, I first saw the shadows on her skin, her face in false submission with the large eyelids loosely closed. And "thank you," she said, and then...

Big Blue Horizon

A CAFE; hot cross buns and acrid coffee. Chrome revolving doors transporting passengers from scalding cold rain to the smooth warmth of the interior. There she stood, all disorientation and curls. She was not in perfect accord with my mind's eye. That pleased me. I was pleased that I could not look into her heart. I knew her past. What should I say?

"I have written you," I could begin, "planned your day, dressed you, fed you, hurried you here."

Such conversational gambits do not work. The truth never really does. I knew of her fear. Her fear of being watched. What was it, she would think, that light that shone on her shoulder?

Play it where it lies – so my brother, Jake, says. My brother Jake, that flux of red face and grinning beard that gives me a sense of home, of safety. Play her where she lies.

From where I lay there was nothing but blue horizon. Maybe my big, hairy brother would write now and then, rest an arm on my shoulder:

"Tell me sis, how are the men in your life treating you?"

Big, blue horizon.

So I see Steve in the bunker, Steve in the water hazard, Stevie the chicken in the rough. Without knowing why, I have this date with Steve, whom I know only from his computer file. He's thirtyish, Latino-Irish, interests include literature and cinema; smokes, drinks, though without excessive relish it would seem.

The Benefits of Tobacco

So the guy, right, creepy but cute, catches me coming through the revolving doors and starts into me with all this girl of his dreams stuff. I mean, I'm not even sure at first if he is my date, my Steve.

She considered this for a moment; considered the point, so finely put, that she was here in the chrome diner to meet her maker. No more, no less.

I told the truth. I was researching my novel, I said, about a man ensnaring his female victims through computer dating. My synopsis had received significantly positive replies, there would be film rights in the offing, the auguries were good. But I was a meticulous man by nature and I felt, and I am sure any great writer would agree (and Papa had preached something similar): the need to write from experience!

"But how?" she asked.

"It's the wanting," I said, immersed in my plot, "the loneliness. And there is his innate charm, the money, the big car..."

She then said something strange:

"You know those American films? Where all the kids are at another film, in their big, sexy cars. Their own cars; all chrome and leather and soft top roof."

"I know, I know. Man, I used love the two page spreads in those American magazines. Those cars! They were always blue and violet with great, predatory chrome grills. And with the airbrushing of the ads they had the deepest, most seductive sheen off their upholstery, like flesh. Empty and big. The page would let you right inside and they were so empty and big."

Oh, she was inside my head now, alright, and I let her in to my dream, my secret. I had written those cars, yes, all of them, all along all the empty highways that stretched to every horizon. They were the big heavy cars that pulled up to the kerb with the window half down and the smoky voice would whisper from the darkness: 'get in'.

She led me on and said, too knowingly: "It's the ultimate teen dream, to have the girl there with you, yes, in the big, blue emptiness of it all. To have the girl with you that was willing. Or, that seemed willing. I mean, really her eyes might not be closed, her eyes might wander over your shoulder and onto the silver screen, her eye might catch the eye of Steve McQueen, or Jimmy Dean."

She was getting the picture. When the cappucinos arrived she went to the ladies. She had been gone a long time when I felt the hand of god on my shoulder.

Out in the alleyway, I'm free. That window in the ladies' was tight but so are my clothes, my too-boyish body. For once in my life no-one is watching. I'm free. Play it as she lies, my brother said to me.

The Apartment Opposite

IN this business there is not a lot to do, so time seeps in from the streets and often, as it ebbs, I float back out there with it, heavy on my hands. There are a lot of things that I can attach myself to, out there in the street. There are men who gather in the scuffed green space where the commercial zone thins before petering out in the back streets. Men who gather there beneath the plane trees and throw boules, or gossip over strong cigarettes and a falling scent of liquorice or cheap aperitif. Sometimes I mingle there and half-heartedly feed the pigeons or mutter agreeable outrage at some recent scandal. But I have never really felt that I fit in there anymore than I've felt that I fit in anywhere. I evoke a faint surprise with any attempted familiarity, as though my face is well enough recognised but the name and character attached not properly recalled, nor do I detect any advance on this situation with the repetition and the passing of time.

The bars and cafes do not engender any more familiarity but at least there conversation and shared secrets are a commonplace. They are even a currency of sorts, a means by which anonymity is briefly exchanged for intimacy, and returned undamaged by the end of the evening.

One time, in an old tobacco bar at the less salubrious end of the street I had a conversation with a woman which gave me that giddy feeling of being known, or that, if followed to a conclusion, we would come to know each other. She had the air of a gypsy, her arms, fingers and throat glistened with ostentatious jewellery, her shirt was colourful and patterned and did little by way of concealment, and her dusky skin was framed by a lustreless tangle of black hair. But enough of that. To return to what was said I recall that, after several drinks, the gypsy woman looked with melancholy yearning into my eyes. Her own eyes were disconcertingly pale.

She asked me if I smoked hashish and I said that I had tried it several times but not since I had graduated from college some dozen years previously. I did not add that what little I had received by way of benefit from the habit was more than offset by feelings of unspecific fear and a tendency towards personal entropy. She was holding my hand in a way that I at first hoped to be a harbinger but now guessed it was just the thing that gypsies do. Then she asked me if I had ever known a man with two different coloured eyes and for a moment I pulsed, but said no.

She was looking at me harder now and withdrew her hand to raise her glass, draining it slowly. "I only ask because it is as well to ask these things first. Before beginning the story," she said, laying heavy emphasis on the emptiness of her glass.

I ordered another round.

It was, she said, a fable told by the semi nomadic people who dawdled and passed through the mountains not far from the coast. Amongst their cargo, more in olden days than now, she insisted, were bales of the best north African hashish. In their mingling with the people of the northern plains several curious mulatto strains developed. Amongst the superstitious the mulatto is often treated with distrust, but where the genetic code bestows features that are manifestly bizarre this can turn to fear.

The Apartment Opposite

A most striking, though rare, condition amongst the mulattos was the condition of having one eye blue and the other brown. As the mulattos were typically traders they were already subject to distrust from both the nomads and the settled peoples, however people with such an affliction were considered especially duplicitous. It would seem, according to the gypsy, that they were the embodiment of the phrase 'two faced'.

I smiled, "That may explain the rarity of the condition," I said.

She shrugged. "Oh, they are there alright, but they have learned how to go unnoticed. It is said," she dropped to a furtive whisper, "that if you smoke hashish with such a man, or even a woman, that you will fall into their eyes and they into yours. That you will no longer have your life as your own, that will be his, while you will be left with the shell of his life."

I know you will think of such talk as hocus pocus, how could one ever believe such things? Still, it makes you wonder. That night I was tempted to stay, imagining a symbiosis which I had not detected before but ultimately I had to opt, once more, for a return to anonymity. And it is not that I have no home to go to.

Every morning I walk the length of the narrow, fourth floor apartment. I sleep in the front on the couch with the noise from the street billowing through the net curtain shielding the balcony. The street can be very loud but seldom so early as to anticipate my awakening. The noise to the rere is less predictable and, too often, tinged with a beckoning aggression. Maria sleeps to the rere, a gorgeous amazon in a storm of white linen. Between us, safe in the painted seascape of her windowless cocoon sleeps our little treasure. Her sighs, so nearly undetectable, are what I search for in the semi darkness of each semi fractured dawn, between sharply raised shutters and the quickly catching blaring of horns, a distant train siren and the first shouted greetings of bakers and binmen and other early birds. There it is, that soft sigh once more, caught like a pause in the day's falling dust.

I am always barefoot as I like the cool feel of the tiles. They run the length of the apartment in a diagonal lock, black and white and subtle as a Vermeer here in the lounge, shimmering like sharkstooth in the distance of the kitchen, gleaming painful silver in the low sun. I know I must make the kitchen although I am keen to keep away. I float past Maria and on out onto the rere balcony where the first subterranean rumblings are already subverting the calm.

Most mornings he's there too.

I am not a voyeur, incidentally. I take no interest in the comings and goings of the demimonde, the inner world enclosed by the city block. A woman tends to a canary one floor down on the connecting street, a disabled music teacher gives tuition one floor up, most nights there are intriguing shadows on the many lit squares that form and float on the impinging darkness, tableau are acted out, sometimes dramatic and at others in tender softness. It mostly washes over me. I seldom sit in living parody of that man in that film, what was it, *Rear Window*; I seldom sit and snoop.

Yet, I am drawn to the rear balcony of the apartment directly opposite. Maybe fifty metres distant, at least not so far as to obliterate all detail. It looks, in overall design, pretty much as I imagine our balcony looks, that uneasy marriage of functionality and elegance, the accumulation of a sepia grime, the French windows and fading shutters. But the apartment opposite does not suffer the chronic clutter that bedevils ours; there is a purposefulness about it and, even at a distance, I can see how well cared for are the plants and, occasionally spying the illuminated interior, how tasteful and warm its ambience.

And there is him. About my own age but slimmer, more athletic of build and mien. Even at the ungodly hour which I habitually rise he seems elegantly pressed and turned out for the day. I strain my eyes to see if he has shaved but, of course, it is impossible to be sure from this distance.

Now, I have noticed that amongst the various effects which are so thoughtfully arrayed around his balcony, there is one which gives me an idea. It is a permanent and prized accoutrement, obviously, its barrel tilted so casually off the vertical but never quite definitely pointed. It is a small telescope. If my neighbour opposite considers it quite alright to have such a device well then – should I not have one of my own?

The telescope brings me much closer but I am nervous about using it when the occupants might be home. I am even shy about displaying it so brazenly in the open as they have done and instead am obliged to skulk – oh, that is too strong a word – I am obliged to operate discretely in the privacy of the kitchen. Even then, I am sensitive to the appearance of my neighbour, his wife or their son at or near the balcony and I desist abruptly, and gaze with sudden interest at the dials on the cooker or some such.

Maria is not well pleased with my new hobby. There is incipient jealousy there, without doubt. She scans the apartments of the caldera honing in on those where she suspects flirtation, or worse.

"That girl could do with the next size up, or forget about clothes at all," she says of one young thing who regularly flaunts her flesh, her fecundity and her foul tongue. Or, "Her there, she would surely get better custom sitting at a front window."

I try to convince her that these sights did not hold me in thrall. "See, there is a fine view of the Jewish quarter and the mount beyond. Come, look, there are fantastic spires."

But she will not.

I fuss over Christina before she heads off for school. She goes to a school nearby close enough for you to hear the children screaming. She wriggles from my embrace but that is the way young girls are. She has gone from the eccentric but beautiful clothes selected by her mother to the plaid and primary uniform of the schoolgirl. Soon she will be clad in the dreary weeds of the teenage generation, perched on benches and corners like famished rooks. For now, though, for now.

"You spoil the girl," Maria says from the shadows, but not without fondness.

I could guess where the apartment was, which at first satisfied me. However, I resolved to put more effort into pinpointing the address exactly. It was simple enough. The avenue ran parallel to ours and I knew the particular block would be central, like mine, and the apartment on the fourth floor, again like mine.

This avenue was on a busy traffic artery unlike the tree-lined pedestrianised rambla which I overlooked. So, although the buildings were similar, turn of the century with that old world attention to detail, there was a busy and bustling patina about his block. I noted that the lobby was enclosed in a double glazed porch whereas ours was behind a wooden door, and there was a lift also where we had to rely on the stairs. I determined to go further and find a name for my shadow.

It was easy to observe the comings and goings in the lobby from a cafe across the street. From there it was a matter of patience and coincidence to discover which of the mailboxes belonged to my man. I was surprised when my heart skipped a beat on seeing him, and skipped another beat as he paused, one afternoon, to nonchalantly check the contents of his postbox. I finished my coffee as slowly as I could and spent some time sauntering along the street before the opportunity arose to gain access to the lobby for a closer look. Beside his bell and the number five was printed his name in an anonymous typewriter font. Mr and Mrs L. Domenech it said. Hardly a biography, but plenty to go on.

The initial and formal title gave it an air of – what? – respectability, I suppose. I was meticulous enough to check it in the phone directory and was rewarded with broadened knowledge. Lionel Domenech it said, but nothing on his wife. Still, when next I viewed my distant neighbour across the caldera of the city block, I could smile with some familiarity and say, there is Mr Domenech, there is Lionel.

I do have my favourite bar, some hundred metres down the rambla towards the ocean. It is called the Theatre bar. Although the theatre opposite has long since given up on showing plays and is now a venue for music and dance, the bar is identified in the traditional way and its sign features two masks, one smiling, one frowning. So, my favourite bar and my favourite barman, Marcos, who, like any emigrant, bore a fond hatred for both his adopted home and his motherland. I liked Marcos because he was one of the few who greeted me, and the only one who knew my order, if not my name. Also, when the mood was jolly he would sneak a quick toast of some burning liquor between orders. Drink, he would order, and we would both knock one back quickly and thump our empties smartly on the counter. Marcos and I were always in harmony.

He had kind words. He would say "You seem gloomy tonight, my friend," or simply, "Cheer up, it is not so bad." There is a danger of becoming maudlin on occasions such as these. There is a danger too of mistaking those token professional kindnesses for something more, for imagining a bond growing where indeed there is nothing more in common than a coincidence of place and time and the necessity of politeness. In time, both dangers would emerge, simultaneously, and provide the inevitable impetus that propels fate.

A couple of nights after my encounter with the gypsy woman I was maudlin in my cups having again had a row with Maria, again concerning my drinking which again, of course, compelled me to go out and drink more. The nights were growing balmy then and I was glad to be able to escape the hubbub of the indoors and sit out on the pavement on the shiny steel chairs, craning up occasionally to catch the sky beyond the tall buildings of the street.

Marcos approaches with my drink. He places it carelessly, but elegantly, on my table. We shoot the breeze briefly and he says something and I smile.

"If you are down, there is something that can lift you up," he says.

I shrug. "It is no matter, we all carry the world, in a way."

Marcos places one foot on the seat beside me and, leaning both arms on the raised knee shakes his head. Slowly, solemnly. "No, my friend, we all carry each other." So saying, he whips out a packet of cigarettes, some exotic brand that I don't recognise, and taking one out places it on top of my packet of Marlboro. It is a strange thing to do and I must look puzzled because he leans closer and offers something by way of explanation. "Enjoy this later, as you stroll home," he says, "and if anyone asks just say it is a foreign cigarette."

Perhaps I am a little naive concerning these things but, as I said, I had smoked hash at college so I am not completely ignorant, and this was a filter cigarette, plain and simple.

I take a long route home sometimes, skirting the lanes of less salubrious areas. There are pleasant boulevards that funnel into lightless canyons, surprising silent squares, sometimes no more than small points of convergence or a cobblestone clearing, the constituent streets radiating outwards like the points of stars. Sometimes I search for the sky, see constellations bisected by gargoyles and spires, then again there are times when what seems like Ursa Major or Cassiopeia is simply the arbitrary arrangement of lights in the apartments of a highrise – a little trick played by the city.

This night I wander more than usual, and I smoke Marcos's cigarette. I envelop myself in the mellow company of tobacco. My feet float across the cobbles. The scents of Africa, India, the South Seas and our own sultry pond seep out of doorways, borne on flickering lights and whispered conversations. Here there is a cacophony where some party spills joking into a cramped alleyway, there two lovers clutch in suspended lust – and dewdrops drip from spider webs and glisten on the ground. At one stage I am surprised to walk into a tableau of a painting by Dali, shadows swathed in robes lounge in shaded corners and an exotic, lonely chant echoes through a cloister. But it is dark and I cannot be sure; I lean forward to tentatively touch the air.

I find myself framed in a darkened doorway. Above at fourth floor level a sheet of light hangs suspended against the night. Projected onto the sheet is the recognisable silhouette of two lovers, recognisable because they are nameable. That is, I can name Lionel because it is his shadow that looms over Mme. Domenech.

I am reminded of a movie, to the extent that I am transported back to my childhood, enraptured in the stalls while above the myriad flickering beams converge on a point, fanning out to form a fantasy. A filigree of smoke sails, effortlessly and perpetually upwards, sewing ghosts and galleons into the fractured darkness. From such a distance I am amazed that Lionel's features are so clear and that, even as I observe what he is doing, he can look beyond his wife's bare shoulder and seek out my eyes.

"You know what must be," he says, in the booming voice of those ancient monochrome movies.

I am distracted by the woman's voice – "No, no, you must not. You can not. Come back to bed."

"It is time," Lionel says, and his face is very close to mine now, somehow. "You know it is time."

I am grievously ill for much of the next morning. I poke at my work in the way I would poke at a plate of unwanted food, if I could bring myself near enough to food to poke at it. Maria has not calmed. She left early for work with little instructions for the day and little apparent concern for my fragile state. Even Christina can seem cruel.

"You smell, Daddy," she says.

"Perhaps it is my Cologne," I say.

She makes a casual oath of disgust.

Yet I smile. She is becoming a young woman. I will lose her anyway.

By the afternoon I am able to stroll the rambla putting the boules players ill at their ease. I have bought bread and cheese and ham for lunch, some of the bread is fed to the pigeons. I am performing the tasks that belong to me but it is as if I have learned them and forgotten why. Christina will eat in silence as she always does, then make some feeble excuse that will send her out spinning into the world again. She will shed her schoolgirl clothes and don something, which, increasingly I will find inappropriate. I have not said so much yet, but she knows that I have thought it. Again I am alone and am drawn to the telescope.

Lionel's wife flits about the apartment, doing, I suppose, the things that women do when alone like that. It is not just ordering things but bestowing them with an aesthetic. It is not, need I add, a thing that Maria indulges overmuch, there is a patina of grime on most things in our apartment, if not physically so then psychologically. In Lionel's apartment, even at this distance, one can see the subtle shine on all the objects and fittings.

At one point there is an extra movement in their living room. A curtain billows and Lionel's wife twirls in an unexpected direction. I see her smile and try to see beyond her shoulder to the shadow that has made her turn. I am reminded of the film noir that I hallucinated last night and I am made even more uneasy. She reaches up to turn down the collar of the intruder but my incipient suspicions are allayed. It is only her son. He is perhaps a year older than Christina and has grown quite tall. I fancy that even in the few short weeks that I have been watching them that I have detected a visible increase in height. The young do everything so quickly. And Lionel's wife is so petite, so charming. If she sends that young boy out in the world, he will return. As will Lionel.

A couple of nights later I am back at the Theatre Bar. I am hoping to see Marcos but he is not on duty. Another waiter, one of his compatriots whose name I do not know, tells me that Marcos may be in the Jewish quarter which he often frequents on his night off.

"Ah," I say, "I understand in your country that is the reverse of the usual procedure."

Either the waiter doesn't get the joke or pretends not to. He leaves with the veiled expression of disdain common to his race and type. Oh well, I shrug to no-one in particular, perhaps he is not yet sufficiently proficient in our language to understand and, of course, the term Jewish has lost all significance in the context of that particular neighbourhood. It is another name marooned from its own meaning, no more descriptive of itself than is the Theatre Bar with its lost connotations of playwrights, impresarios and thespians.

I finish my drink and walk into the maelstrom of the city night. I try to retrace my steps of the other night but there is no magic in it and no visions of strangeness emerge. What once appeared to me as exotic tableau are now revealed as little more than the arbitrary thinning or thickening of crowds, drawn by conspiracies no more mysterious than the magnets of commerce, marked less by the elegant strangeness of ethnicity than by the desperation of incipient squalor. After an hour I feel the city close in on me and, simultaneously, recede from me so that it twists into a vast and teeming dungeon, such light that hits its floor coming from barred windows set at an unimaginable height. At last I stop at a kiosk for a kebab and a coffee, leaning on a metal counter with unshaven and swarthy men who barely conceal their surly interest in my presence.

As I am almost finished, the coincidence which I await occurs. On the steps of a scaffolded building I spy Marcos remonstrating with two men. They are some twenty metres distant but I can tell that the three are acquainted though not in a comradely sense. Marcos abruptly breaks from the group and stalks into the dark mouth of a laneway. The two men, one suited and the other wearing a startling white shirt, throw stagelike gestures and then follow. I too spring in that direction, still clutching the remains of my kebab.

There is an outbreak of sullen anger behind me and I half turn and see the moustachioed proprietor sprint from his kiosk and close the ground between us with alacrity and, more alarmingly, the augmentation of a couple of eager deputies. I had neglected to pay! As I am seized I pull a note from my pocket which the proprietor grabs with an oath. It is far too much for the foul snack I had suffered but I judge there is little point awaiting my change and there are more important matters pressing.

"Keep the change," I say with an attempted sneer but laughter and more oaths rebound off my back as I make for the laneway. The entrance is narrow and dark before opening into an empty bottle of an urban clearing. This is a long narrow cobbled rectangle flanked on each side by cloisters with a begrimed Palladian portico at the far end and the silhouette of a tower rising vaguely behind it. At first it seems empty then I see shadows flit and scuffle in the cloisters to my right. I run towards the fracas, the softness of my footfalls further hidden by the shouts of the men and the solid thumping of blows.

The only role open to me was that of hero, a role I had only ever played before inside my head. I doubt that the first guy I tackled knew what hit him. At first I wasn't terribly sure myself. I can only vouch for the effectiveness of my intervention, not its finesse.

The besuited one bears the brunt of my attack, his head jolts back and a shower of bloody matter sprays across his comrade's white shirt; the latter is transfixed and stands with his arms spread and mouth open. Only then did I notice that I still clutched the remains of the wretched kebab.

At our ease later with the assailants flown, Marcos laughs. We sit on the steps of the forgotten church and attempt to clean ourselves of blood and, mostly, kebab.

"I thought you had knocked his brains out," he says, "then I remembered Eduard doesn't have any brains."

"You knew him, so?"

Marcos moves to blur his indiscretion. "Ah, can we ever truly know anyone?"

"But he is a friend?"

"No, no, a compatriot, yes; but this is no longer the patria. Ah, the fields where we grew and where we played, where we thought we would oneday die. Perhaps we bring some shadow of them with us when we come to a different city, but only a shadow. Back then, my friend, we were fierce in our recognition of ourselves, of each other and of our own. Alas, we are now chameleons. You know the chameleon?"

I tell him yes, it is a creature that takes on the colour and texture of its surroundings, that it is perfectly camouflaged from its predators and its prey.

"Yes," Marcos says, "to all intents it is invisible. For immigrants like us that is the necessary condition, we are 'obviously invisible' if you like – but I think there is a little of the chameleon in us all." Marcos pauses, examining the handkerchief I have given him to clean some blood off his lip. He runs his thumb along the monogram. "So, Eduard, I know him and I don't know him. There is history between us but it never ends. I often wonder why this man, this Eduard, carries a name and identity which I can no longer reconcile. While you, my friend, I don't even know your name."

I demur. "I can hardly expect you to. Yours I know, because it is always 'Marcos, bring me a drink' or 'where is the menu, Marcos?'"

"You are not the worst."

"You asked can we ever know anyone. What is most difficult is to truly know oneself. Perhaps that is why we are forever trying to be someone other than who we are."

"You are deep, my friend." Marcos folds the handkerchief and I hold up my palm to stay its return. He puts it apologetically in his jacket pocket and takes out a packet of cigarettes, offering me one. "The man with no name, eh?"

"My name? It is Lionel, Lionel Domenech."

"Well, Lionel." Marcos places undue emphasis on the name. From his pocket he takes out a small, slim phial of dark liquid. "Regarde – oil of hashish, the herb in its most potent essence." He unscrews the cap which has a pointer attached and he slides this along the seam of his cigarette then, with a light grip on my hand, he repeats the application on my own.

I use my lighter and we smoke in scented silence for a while. The distant sky is illuminating and exploding with arbitrary intensity but it seems impossibly distant from the hidden cobblestone square. Marcos holds the phial out to me. Again I raise a palm in polite refusal but Marcos shakes his head and places the phial emphatically in my left breast pocket.

"Think of it as a route map – if you want to remember who you are perhaps this will help you to know where to look. Too often we think that we are, each of us, an island, but look here," and he pats my pocket again, "and you will see that there are connections between everyone and everything."

It is a long walk home. It is the feast of St John and all along the Esplanade people gather and crush long into the night. Fireworks rain upwards into the sky clapping and barking between the glass towers along the seafront. Even at this late hour children scurry across the dusty playing fields, shrieking as firecrackers skip between their shadows. I descend to the beach where the sand flows like silk over my plimsolls. At a much later hour I am dancing in unison with scores of strangers as a strobe light stutters and a trance like beat pulses across the sand and into the dark swollen water. I think I will never go home, I think this will last forever.

Now that I follow Lionel regularly I feel there is a distinct bond between us. At the same time I am anxious lest I be discovered. I would say Lionel is a careful man. His suits are well pressed. He walks with a studied grace and takes due notice of all those things city life has to offer – stopping to view a window display here, greeting an acquaintance there, elsewhere smiling at some incident amongst children in the park. I find myself copying these actions without really meaning to. I am aware that an objective observer might see this and suspect, but I console myself that there is no objective observer.

It is summer now and the city is speckled with impressionistic colour, the pavements are a blinding terrazzo of reflected sunlight and dappled shade and everywhere the citizens are shedding their dour suits of spring and winter for an altogether edgier plumage. I become strictly downbeat at this time of year, much to Maria's chagrin – faded Chinos and open sandals, a teeshirt that is offwhite more through weariness than intent. Lionel changes only subtly – the sleeves of his pastel shirts are short, his fashionable strides are lighter and his shoes less aggressively shiny. I buy some shirts in Carrefour of the type he prefers. Maria is suspicious to see me wearing them one morning.

"Have you got an interview?" she asks.

I shrug. "What is so wrong with wearing something nice on such a nice day?"

"I didn't say there was anything wrong," she says, and summons clouds into the blue sky. Again she leaves the house dissatisfied and again I wonder if Lionel has to suffer so much from his wife. It seems unlikely. She is so petite and, even at a distance, I can see she is graced with a permanent smile. These thoughts do not balm me and I feel harried and oppressed as I step out onto the rambla my mood only lifting as I turn into Lionel's street.

The Benefits of Tobacco

There is hardly any need to stalk him now so well do I know his route and his admirably predictable timetable. On such a humid morning as this has become I know I will find him on the terrace of the Goya Cafe. It is already filling up when I get there with people attracted to the cones of shade cast by the giant orange parasols.

I sit directly across from Lionel at the corner where the cafe curves into a side street. We are so close that I feel quite giddy. He is drinking an americano and does not seem to notice me. After some minutes he pats his breast and then his trouser pockets, then he glances at me. His expression is rueful and apologetic. I thrill to the current of anticipation – will he recognise me? Something else makes my heart skip a beat and it is so unlikely that at first I cannot name the thought.

"A curse on it," he says with an easy smile, "I have forgotten them?"

I know what he means but my reply is stalled by the surprise: Lionel's eyes are handsome and bright as I knew they would be but I could not have guessed that one would be blue and the other brown.

Lionel frowns slightly, "My cigarettes," he says and gives a nonchalant shrug.

The feeling snaps back to my extremities and I force a smile. Not so forced, in fact; as soon as the aberration was witnessed the plan hit me, manifest in its obvious simplicity. "Have one of mine," I say and I flip my pack to him.

Lionel politely demurs. "Ah, but you have only two left, I will ask..."

I stop him with a wave of my hand. "Nonsense, what good is hoarding?" I remember Marcos, "Come," I say,

"Don't let us be islands."

We smoke together in quiet companionship. We are like two old friends who meet here with familiar regularity. What is said? I cannot say. It drifts upwards with the smoke through the canopy of leaves and merges seamlessly with the endless and endlessly thinning air. Circling birds anticipate their migration and climb in the updrafts, looking down now and then to notice nothing at all.

The cafe empties of its morning rush and time slows imperceptibly. One table to the side remains occupied where two men, quite similar from afar, sit over their empty cups. Who is to say which of the two men leaves first. Afterwards even they themselves will be unclear on that detail. There is no pressing engagement for either to attend to but, against that, there is a certain loosening in the molecular attraction that existed between them and both find themselves subsumed in diverging currents that flow off into the city.

A fog materialised that morning, slowly infecting the air. It came from no particular direction or, at least, from no discernible place out there. This tangible manifestation of atmosphere came from within, an insidious subversion of the air seeping up from the drains and cellars of the city. People were caught in it like flies on sticky paper, poised above the pavements in a gross parody of urban bustle.

As he turned into his street he heard the buzz grow in imperceptible increments, like some approaching swarm, still some way off but already incomprehensibly large. Out here on the street he felt as if he were on a treadmill and that, most likely, this created the illusion of stasis amongst the hurrying throng. We're all marking time, he thought, and getting nowhere. This condition of stasis persisted throughout the day, if indeed a day could be said to pass with such a complete absence of movement.

Lionel was unwilling to seek an alternative, it was not an eternity although not far off nor could he admit the possibility that it was an instant. No, it was a day and then with the onset of evening it dispersed, almost abruptly. Lionel caught the surreptitious stares of the stragglers left striving for home, exchanging tendrils of unformed guilt, barely whispered promises. Tell no one. We will not tell.

Lionel Domenech awoke and walked across the cool tiles to the kitchen at the rere. His small family slept. The boy, now almost a man, snored in his own room. The woman – for long no longer a girl – slept soundlessly in a storm of white silk. Last night he had made love to her as if for the first time and had triggered a trepidation that it might soon be the last. Why did that thought lodge there?

Lionel looked out from his rear balcony, looked out towards the apartment directly opposite. Lately he had noticed that his son sometimes pointed the small telescope in that direction. The father had supposed this to be evidence of awakening desire inspired, no doubt, by the vision of a young girl and was amused, but this morning he was not so sure. He saw a movement there, as he had sometimes sensed movement before, but most likely it was just the breeze drifting a curtain. Clouds billowed beyond the roofline and there was the sudden collective hush of approaching rain. The weather was changing and with it the city and all that dwelt there. Welling up within him, Lionel felt an overwhelming sense of sadness.